HIM

JONNI ANDERSON

Starwatch Creations
Orange Park, Florida

Starwatch Creations
Orange Park, Florida

For Hansel:
Blue skies, my friend, fair winds.
I'll see you on the other side.

My Thanks. . .

Writing a book is a learning process. I've read many novels set in the eras I write about here, but reading them isn't the same as writing them. Suddenly little details I skimmed over when I was reading assumed paramount importance when I was writing, and I realized I didn't have the answers. Others did—friends like Ika Santamaria, Barbara Goldman and Helen M. Rake. My thanks to you all—and especially to Scott Jones, who provided line-by-line editing and cover design.

Any remaining mistakes are entirely my own.

Thank you, my friends! I learned a lot from all of you!

HIM

JONNI ANDERSON

1

I should have run the first time I saw him.

The lighting in the hotel's grand ballroom was muted for the gala, but the diamonds flashing in the dimness were not. Governor Rossini's wife, looking like a jewelry store advertisement — I wondered snidely where she'd parked her sandwich board — chatted with Bernard LeCoeur, the movie star hunk. Off-screen, he looked like a prosperous, bespectacled insurance salesman. Across the room, Mayor Johnson and his wife held court — but I noticed the woman rumored to be Johnson's current mistress was present, too, on the arm of a man who looked as if he'd be happier chugalugging boilermakers and arm-wrestling with Bubba at the corner pub. Perhaps wifey would be a good girl and go home early so the mayor could have himself a little extra-marital fun.

God, I thought, *there's enough wealth in this room to feed everybody in the country for a year. So what am I doing here?*

Then I saw him. Lounging against the bar, surveying the crowd with a supercilious smile, he looked strange-

ly familiar, but I couldn't place him. Although the gala
was a black-tie do, he wore a Shakespearean-style open-
necked white silk poet's tunic with billowing sleeves.
No tie, black or otherwise. His long dark hair, curling
slightly at the ends, was caught neatly at the nape of his
neck with a silver clasp, heightening the Shakespearean
effect. He seemed to shimmer. I couldn't take my eyes
off him, and when our eyes met — as, I realized later,
they were destined to do — I was lost in a vortex of forces
that snatched the air from my lungs and slammed my
heart into overdrive. The bartender said something to
him and he threw his head back and laughed, a full, happy sound that made everyone around him smile.

Somehow I remembered to breathe.

As I eased through the crowd he watched me with a
mischievous smile — a cat watching a mouse. If he'd had
a tail, it would have twitched. Abruptly he put his drink
down and moved toward me, his smile widening. "Darling! You're late! Where have you been?"

Stunned, I struggled for a snappy retort — but the
excited confusion turned to embarrassment when he
walked past me into the arms of a woman behind me.
I pretended indifference as they moved to a far corner
where they stood talking, heads intimately together. I
had to admit they made an attractive couple, both tall
and dark-haired, slim and graceful. She wore a Kelly
green sheath which revealed nothing and promised everything; a small tiara sparkled in her short dark hair.
In response to something he said, she kissed him on the
cheek, then threw her arms around him.

Flustered and strangely irritated, I turned to look for
Ron, who stood near the patio windows staring morose-
ly at the snow swirling outside. I wondered again what
he saw in me, a half-breed *Latina*, but I had to admit he
was everything I had ever dreamed of. Tall and almost
too good-looking, with a perfect tan, sandy hair and that
aristocratic aura of one raised in wealth, he wore his tux-

edo as if he'd been born in one. He was a native of Miami, and had never been comfortable with the northern climate or culture. I knew from his expression he was thinking of home. He saw my reflection in the glass and turned to smile. "I thought you'd gotten lost in the blizzard."

"You must be a Southerner! That's not a blizzard, that's a light dusting of snow."

"Huhney, ahm all Southeneh when it comes to this hyere whaht stuff." Dropping the exaggerated drawl, he added, "Do you know that's frozen water? That means it's cold enough to freeze water out there!"

I laughed. "Oh, my dear man, you have a lot to learn about winter."

He shook his head. "If there's gonna be white stuff on the ground, I want nice white sand on a nice warm tropical beach where the only frozen water is the ice in my margarita."

"Daphne!" It was Stan Bennett, balding, chubby, rumpled, his eye glasses as always askew.

"Stan! I didn't expect to see you here." I gave him a quick peck on the cheek and turned to Ron. "Ron McIntyre, I'd like you to meet Stan Bennett, the man who helped me get Country Cuzzin started." Stan's company had given me a lot of free advertising in exchange for an exclusive on certain Country Cuzzin lines, and I considered him a good friend as well as a colleague.

"I've heard a lot about you," Stan grinned as they shook hands. "Daphne seems to think you're something very special."

Ron gave him that slow grin I thought of as his Charming Southern Executive smile. "I think she's something special, too."

"Just between us, I agree. You've got yourself quite a lady here. She's always been up front with me, done exactly what she said she'd do. It's a pleasure to do business with her. I suggest you keep her."

Ron put an arm around my shoulders and replied, "Actually, I've been seriously considering it."

Stan gave me a quick hug and disappeared into the crowd, saying he had had enough high-society hype and was going home to his wife.

Ron said something to me, but suddenly my head was filled with a roaring, like an oncoming hurricane. From the corner of my eye, I saw *him* again. Without turning my head, I knew he was watching me — I swear I could *feel* his stare, a full-power force-field. Something warm engulfed me, like a blanket of super-heated air. I gasped, my head reeling. Ron's arm tightened to steady me. "Hey, you okay?"

"Uh . . . I . . . I think so. . ."

"Let's find you a place to sit down." Full of concern and southern gallantry, he led me toward a chair. I was embarrassed and annoyed with myself for my inexplicable urge to run from — to? — that questioning, mocking smile across the room, and I tried to assure Ron I was fine. But he insisted I stay put while he rushed off to find a glass of water. I'd rather have had wine, but the poor man needed to feel useful.

I felt rather than saw *him* approach. I didn't dare look up, but he stood so close I thought I could feel his warmth. All I could see were his low-cut boots and trousers that flared slightly at the bottom.

"Your friend seems concerned," he murmured. "Are you all right?" Voice low and gentle — *warm honey and black velvet, alto sax at 4:00 a.m., smoke-filled bar, bourbon straight up, a hint of amusement* — a voice to drown in. . .

I looked up. Our eyes met, and I saw his widen in surprise, for we were suddenly alone in a silent world that thrummed with electricity and the promise of high winds to come. I could actually *feel* him inside my head. I wanted to throw myself into his arms; I wanted to run; I wanted . . .

"Excuse me. . ."

It was Ron, holding a glass of water, glancing from me to Shakespeare, questions in his eyes.

"Oh, thank you, Ron. Uh . . . this is . . ." *This is a man I've never met whom I've known for millennia, who haunts my dreams and just stole my soul and if he doesn't move away I'm going to scream!*

Shakespeare recovered from his own trance and, smiling affably, offered Ron his hand. "I'm Trevor Elliot. Your friend looked rather upset and I was concerned." There was the slightest hint of an accent but I couldn't place it. *Honey and black velvet. . .* I shivered.

Ron shook hands, eyeing Elliot warily. "Ron McIntyre. Thanks — I think she'll be all right. She's been under a lot of stress lately."

The Shakespearean enigma named Trevor Elliot turned to me and extended his hand. I expected the conventional handshake, but instead he bowed low and kissed my hand with ancient gallantry, then smiled into my eyes. Something shot up my arm and burned all the way down to my toes. *Bourbon straight up. . .* "Perhaps we'll meet again," he murmured, then, nodding to Ron, he turned and strolled over to his wife — companion? — significant other? Why did I envy her so? And why was I trembling?

Ron turned back to me. "Where did you meet that guy?"

"What? Oh — I haven't — I mean, I didn't. He just walked up and asked if I was okay."

"You were staring at each other like long-lost lovers."

"Were we? I guess it's the way he's dressed. He reminds me of somebody but I can't think who."

"I don't like him."

"For heaven's sake, Ron! You just met the man."

"I didn't like the way he was looking at you."

No wonder — he was reading my mind, probing to the depths of my psyche, taking me prisoner, and I was helpless to stop him. . . I clasped my hands in my lap to hide their trembling and tried not to stare after him.

I didn't speak with Trevor Elliot again that evening, but I was aware of him. No matter where I went, he was within range. It was apparent he was well known, for there was always a small crowd around him. A couple of times our eyes met and locked, but then one of us reluctantly broke the connection. And sometimes his strangely familiar laugh taunted me from across the room. I realized I hadn't told him my name. How could I remedy that? And what good would it do? — for his lovely companion stuck quite close to him the rest of the evening, and it was apparent they were very fond of each other. At one point I was positive he was telling her about me; I saw her glance surreptitiously in my direction, then quickly away, a smile on her face. I pictured them in bed later that night, laughing at the peculiar *Latina* wallflower with the rich dude from the South.

I felt my face flush. *I'm a mature, successful 32-year-old businesswoman! I've paid my dues on the romance circuit and I don't need this sleazy exhibitionist and his fancy woman making fun of me!*

I had to regroup. "Excuse me, Ron. I'm going to find the ladies' room."

Instead I stood in shadows on the mezzanine, surveying the crowd below, trying to pretend I wasn't looking for Trevor Elliot.

A woman joined me at the railing. "The Harmons put on quite a gala."

It was Elliot's woman, she of the Kelly green sheath, taller than I by several inches, smiling faintly.

Curiosity overcame my irritation, and, instead of turning haughtily away, I replied, "I find myself wondering what they expect to accomplish. This must cost a fortune."

"Oh, I suspect they'll find a way to make it a tax write-off." She smiled and offered her hand. "I'm Sylvia

Elliot. I'm an interior decorator."

"Daphne Morris. I don't quite know how I would classify myself. I guess I'm an importer."

"Sounds exotic. What do you import?"

"A line of hand-made rustic household furnishings and decorations which we market under the name Country Cuzzin."

Her eyes widened with new interest. "I've heard of you. You have a reputation for carrying quality stuff."

"We carry only authentic, first-class merchandise — or try to. We've done pretty well, I think." I hoped I sounded modestly casual.

"You know, this may be an answer to prayer. We just won a rather large contract — large for us. We'll be doing all the interior decoration for the LakePointe resort."

"On the south shore? They really planned big, didn't they?"

She nodded. "They want luxury with a rustic ambience; I think your product line might be perfect."

"It would certainly be worth discussing. Maybe we should do lunch or something."

She handed me her card and I fumbled for my own, grateful I had, for once, remembered to put some in my handbag.

"I'll call you week after next, if that's all right," she said. "We have final planning meetings with the developers next week, and by then I should have a fair idea of what I'll need."

"Sounds great."

"I think this could be good for both of us. Now I must run. It was great talking with you."

On the drive home, Ron's adrenaline kept him prattling. "Did you enjoy yourself? An interesting mix of people there, didn't you think?"

My thoughts were far away. *Who the hell was that Elliot guy — married to a stunning woman like that — making eyes at me? And what did those eyes of his do to me? Every time he looked at me, my knees went rub-bery and my brain quit working. . . Where's that alto sax coming from? . .*

"Daphne? You awake?"

"What? Oh, yes, it was nice. Thank you for inviting me."

"Mighty Millicent was there. Did you see her?"

"Who?"

"Millicent Dwyer, the senator's bitch of a wife," he replied. "She actually deigned to talk with me. I may have a good chance at her account — she's not happy with the travel agency she's with now, and I'm to call her next week."

"That's nice." *Dammit, I'm a grown woman! So why am I acting like a hormone-jazzed adolescent with the hots for some refugee from the Three Musketeers? Him with his superior smile and grand gestures! Warm honey. . .*

I reached over to turn the volume up on the radio, but it was off.

"Do you want the radio on?" Ron asked.

"What? Oh, I thought it was on; I keep hearing an alto sax."

There was a long silence. Finally Ron asked, "You've been distracted all evening. Are you okay?"

"Sure. Just have a lot on my mind." *And what was darling Sylvia up to? Checking out the competition — or is she into procurement? I'm sorry I gave her my card. . . Bourbon and black velvet. . .*

At my door, Ron kissed me on the forehead and turned to leave. "Sleep well," he murmured. "I'll give you a call tomorrow."

"Aren't you coming in?" I'm not sure which of us was more surprised. Why had I said that, when I really want-ed to be alone with my confusion?

He hesitated. "You seem pretty worn out. I thought I should let you get to bed."

"Come in for a few minutes anyhow. Fix yourself a drink. I'll be down in a minute."

To this day I cannot explain what I did next. I had planned on slipping into jeans and a shirt. Instead, I dug in my closet for a virtually transparent black negligee, unused since my divorce. *Well, why not?* I rationalized. *Ron's a nice guy, and I've been keeping him at a distance long enough.*

The expression on his face when I sauntered barefoot down the stairs filled me with malicious satisfaction. His eyes widened and he spluttered into his drink.

"My god, Daphne. . ."

I pirouetted. "Do you like it?"

Ragged whisper: "Who the hell wouldn't? Are you sure about this?"

I took the drink out of his hand, pressed myself against him, and kissed him, long, slow and thoroughly. I could feel his swelling, and, stifling second thoughts, I unbuttoned his shirt and worked my tongue down his chest. He groaned, and then he was helping me, clothes flying in every direction.

Suddenly we were rolling on the floor, tearing at each other. Once or twice he struggled for control, but I subdued him with urgent, smothering kisses and busy hands.

Much later I lay naked on top of him on the sofa, panting and exhausted, in a tangle of clothing and pillows. Still wearing his silk executive socks, he caressed my back, murmuring, "Where'd that come from?"

I shrugged and said nothing, because the truth was too painful: I hadn't been making love to Ron McIntyre. I had been trying exorcize the mocking, green-eyed ghost of Trevor Elliot, a man who I knew — just plain *knew* — had haunted me since the beginning of time. His face floated behind my eyelids. *Black velvet. . .* I burst into tears.

Ron was immediately contrite. "Oh, darling, did I

hurt you? I didn't mean to! I'm so sorry!"

Suddenly I hated him — hated the sound of his voice, the touch of his hand, the smell of his cologne — hated myself for what I'd done, hated him for allowing it to happen. I put my hand over his mouth, knowing that if he said another word I'd gouge his eyes out and try to strangle him. "No, I'm fine," I stammered. "I guess I'm tireder than I thought."

"Would you like me to leave?"

I sighed. "It might be best, Ron. I'm pretty confused right now."

"Are you sure you should be alone?"

"I'll be okay." Trembling, I stood up, aware of my bruises, filled with humiliation and guilt, terrified of the rage inside me. I pulled a sofa blanket around me, struggling for some vestige of dignity.

My god, I raped the stupid bastard and he's too dumb to know it!

Ron dressed quickly, then put his arms around me. "Get some sleep. This was right for both of us, sweetheart; I think we both got some questions answered. I hope you're not sorry it happened. You sure I didn't hurt you?"

I shook my head. "I'm fine." *Liar!*

He tried to kiss me but I turned my head; I had all I could do to keep from belting him.

"I'll call you tomorrow, okay?" he murmured.

Will you just get the goddam hell out of here?

I gave him a perfunctory kiss, locked the door behind him, then threw myself on my bed and screamed into the pillow, pounding my fists against the wall. My rage propelled me off the bed. Grabbing the first thing I touched — a bottle of expensive perfume Ron had given me — I heaved it at the mirror. The thunder of shattering glass was infinitely satisfying, and somehow shocked me back to sanity — but the overwhelming scent made me retch. What was happening to me? Had I gone around the bend? I had always been a rather passive person, and this sudden violence scared me. I fell back on the bed, sobbing. Somewhere an alto sax sobbed with me.

I knew only one thing for certain: whoever Trevor-be-damned-Elliot was, he had triggered something deep and ugly in me.

And I didn't know how to put the demon back in the bottle.

2

The knock on the door was soft, tentative. "Who would be calling at this hour on Shabbat?" I whispered. "Not the SS; they always come in the middle of the night and it's only a little after sundown."

My husband Mordecai gestured for me to open the door. "And they never knock that softly! It's probably that woman next door wanting a cup of sugar or something. Intrusive pest!"

But it was the SS! I backed away in horror as the tall man entered the room in his impeccably tailored black SS Stürmbannführer's uniform, the silver death's head glinting on his peaked cap. And then I recognized him: Kurt Hartkopf, blond and blue-eyed, once a friend of our son Chaim.

Kurt held up his hands reassuringly. "I haven't come to arrest you. I remember what Chaim did for me, and I've come to warn you. They're relocating all the Jews to camps in the north, Herr Guzmann. You must get out — now!"

My husband, in his sixties, arthritic and stooped, still

wearing his Shabbat yarmulke, put his arm around my shoulders and replied quietly, "We have many friends here. There is nothing to fear."

"Your friends will turn against you! They have to, to save themselves! You must leave! It may already be too late!"

"My son. . ."

"Don't call me that! I'm not your son!" He raised his chin, his blue eyes flashing. "In spite of the fact that Chaim saved my life, I'm a pure Aryan and a proud member of the Nazi party! I'm risking my life and yours by coming here to warn you. I can't come here again. Go now! Take what you can carry in your pockets and run!" Then he dashed down the stairs and disappeared into the night.

Fearfully, I turned to my husband. "Maybe he's right, Mordecai. Maybe we should leave. You know how all the others have disappeared. . ."

"Now, now, Deborah, don't fret so. I have a respect-ed position at the university, and you know God will protect us. He has always looked out for His people, and He won't fail us now."

"But Kurt. . ."

". . . has made his choice," Mordecai answered firm-ly. "We can do nothing for him, nor he for us. I warned Chaim this would happen. Come now, libling, it's time for mint tea and honey cake. You make such delicious cake!"

Much later that night we were jerked awake by an imperious pounding on the door.

❧   ❦

I awoke screaming, tangled in the sheets, soaked with perspiration. Trembling and disoriented, I turned on the lamp and stared blankly around the room for sev-eral minutes before I understood I was in my own home in twenty-first century America, not in a cramped apartment in Nazi Germany. The dream had been so *real!*

Shivering, I pulled on a robe and stumbled to the kitchen to make a cup of tea. I had heard that dreams were supposed to be messages from our subconscious, but this one defied my inept analysis, and, coming as it did after the . . . *incident* . . . with Ron made me suspect it wasn't coincidence. The tea grew cold in front of me while I tried to figure it out.

I didn't know much about a war that had ended long before I was born, but I'd always thought that back then Germans and Jews hated each other. Why would Kurt, a German Nazi, risk his life to warn a couple of aging Jews? And why was Kurt so proud of the fact he was an Aryan? According to my dictionary, Aryan was a Mideastern race. If he was a blond and blue-eyed German, how could he be Iranian or whatever?

But what unnerved me the most was that, although none of the characters in the dream looked like anyone I knew, I somehow *knew* that Mordecai was Ron and Kurt was Trevor. The Trevor I had met at the party was, I guessed, in his early or middle thirties; dark-haired with dark green eyes. This Trevor — Kurt — had been taller, more powerfully built, blond with cornflower-blue eyes, in his early twenties. Yet they were somehow the same person. And Mordecai, in his sixties (as I had been in the dream) looked nothing like Ron, who was 38. Neither Ron nor I had any Jewish blood in us, at least as far as I knew. It made no sense.

Why had I awakened with such a feeling of impending horror? Was this some sort of warning about my getting too involved with Ron McIntyre? Or just a confused reaction to the night's savagery?

Afraid to go back to sleep, I stared mindlessly at the TV until the sun rose and I felt safe enough to turn off the telephone ringer and fall asleep on the couch.

❧   ❦

Jerked awake by the doorbell's insistent jangling, I screamed, "Mordecai! Gestapo! They've found us!" But it was Ron, on the verge of hysteria. I was amazed at the rush of rage I felt.

"Daphne! Are you all right? I've been calling for hours!" He pushed past me into the entryway and turned to wrap his arms around me.

"I'm fine, Ron. Please — you're suffocating me!"

He let go of me, but kept his hands on my shoulders, studying me. "Are you sure you're okay? Why didn't you answer your phone?"

"I turned off the ringer when I went to bed. I guess I forgot you were going to call."

Following me into the kitchen, he said, "I didn't want to call too early because I know you like to sleep late, but when it got to be noon and you didn't answer your phone, I got worried. By the time 2:00 came around, I was about out of my mind."

"Two o'clock? Is it that late?"

"It's nearly three now."

"I'm sorry I worried you. I had a bad dream and didn't get back to sleep until well after dawn."

He regarded me for a long moment. "Are you upset by what happened last night?"

I sighed. "I . . . I don't know. . . I've apparently passed through some kind of door or barrier. I'm not the same person I was twenty-four hours ago, and I don't know what it means or what to do about it."

He put his arm around my shoulders and I shuddered, remembering Mordecai's same gesture, and pulled away. "Do you hear that?"

"Hear what?"

"Somebody's playing an alto sax. Where's it coming from? I don't have a radio on. . ."

"I don't hear anything." Ron eyed me suspiciously.

"Are you sure you're okay?"

My hand jerked toward a butcher knife on the counter. It would be so easy . . . his blood all over the kitchen . . . Trembling, I back away. *A sax moaned about bourbon straight up . . .*

"You're *not* okay!" he said. "I shouldn't have let it happen."

"I don't know, Ron — I just don't know. Frankly, I'm scared. Suddenly I don't know myself, and I don't trust myself." Tears stung my eyes. "I'm supposed to be a well-balanced, successful businesswoman, and for the past twenty-four hours I've been acting like a nut case!"

As he moved to put his arms around me again, I shoved him away. "I think you'd better go."

"Daphne darling, we need to talk," he said gently. "Fix yourself a cup of tea and sit down here with me."

Somehow the fireplace poker was in my hand and I swung it at his head, imagining with delight his brains splattered all over the carpet. But he stepped out of range and stared at me. "Daphne! For god's sake!"

Warm honey. . . smoke-filled bar. . . Out of control now, I attacked in earnest. I managed to land a solid blow to his forearm, but he took it and stepped inside my next swing to wrest the poker from me.

"What the hell's the matter with you! Daphne!"

I pulled out of his grasp and grabbed the butcher knife. "It's your fault!" I screamed, stabbing at him. "If it hadn't been for you we wouldn't be here!"

"What the hell are you talking about?" Ron evaded my attack and headed for the door. I was right behind him, my arm raised to stab again. But again he was faster than I was, and, turning, managed to grab both my wrists. He twisted my knife arm behind me and pulled. "Drop it, dammit! Drop it or I'll break your arm!" To emphasize his threat, he pulled upward on my arm. I screamed and dropped the knife.

And abruptly I was sane again. I sagged in his grasp

and sobbed, but he didn't lessen the pressure on my arm.

"Are you going to settle down?" he demanded.

Wearily I nodded.

He held me for a moment longer to assure himself I wouldn't attack again, then turned me around to face him. I became aware my bare feet were icy on the tile floor.

"Talk to me, Daphne."

I shook my head.

"What did you mean that it's all my fault?" he demanded.

"What?"

"You said it was all my fault. Are you talking about last night?"

"What?" I was confused and bone-deep tired.

"*What* is all my fault?" he said again.

"I don't know what you're talking about," I sobbed.

"You said a few minutes ago that it was all my fault, that if it hadn't been for me we wouldn't be here. Be *where*? And what in god's name is my fault? I need some answers, Daphne. And I need them now."

"I didn't say that."

"Yes you did. Just as you swung at me."

I rubbed my face. "I don't remember saying anything. I just remember your threatening to break my arm."

"You hit me with the poker and then tried to stab me."

"I did not!"

Ron pulled up his sleeve, where a huge bruise was already turning a ghastly purple. "Why do you think I threatened to break your arm?" He pointed to the butcher knife still lying on the floor. "You were about to kill me."

Then it all came back to me in a hideous rush. I burst into sobs again. "Oh, god, Ron, I'm sorry! I don't remember a thing except your telling me we needed to talk."

Ron was silent for a long moment. "What do you want me to do, Daphne? This is a side of you I never knew existed. I thought I knew you pretty well, but frankly I'm beginning to have some doubts."

I nodded. "So am I." I raised my head and looked at him; his blond hair was still in place, but his face was full of doubt and fear. "All I can say is I'm sorry, Ron. It's such a stupid cliché, but I can only say I don't know what came over me."

"Have you ever done this before?"

"To anyone else? No, I swear it! I'm as scared as you are!" And indeed I realized I was shivering. I pulled a blanket off the couch and wrapped it around me, but it didn't help the shivering.

"What do you want me to do?" he repeated softly.

"I don't know! I don't know anything!" I wailed. "Maybe I just need to be alone for a while."

"I'm afraid to leave you alone, but I'm afraid to stay," he replied. "And I don't trust you. I'm afraid you'll do yourself harm."

I shook my head. "I won't, I promise. I guess I need to figure some things out."

"I'm no psychiatrist, but I think you might be heading for some sort of crisis. Maybe you should get some help."

"It's been a busy few weeks; I guess I'm tired, and I think I'm about due for my period," I answered lamely. "Please don't worry — I'll be fine."

He tried to argue, but I hurried him out, promising to call if I felt the slightest need to talk. Then I collapsed against the locked door, still shivering and crying, horrified by compulsions I couldn't understand.

But suddenly I realized I had work to do. After deleting all eight of his messages on the answering machine, I tossed the pillows and throw from the couch in the washing machine, scrubbed floors, cleaned up the glass from the shattered mirror, vacuumed every millimeter of the house. In spite of the winter temperatures, I turned off the heat and opened all the windows to let fresh, cold air in. Bundled in a heavy sweater and jeans, I filled the dishwasher with every glass I thought he might have touched. I washed windows and every piece of clothing I'd worn last night. Then I sterilized the bathroom. I even polished furniture, pretending I wasn't erasing fingerprints, but I knew exactly what I was doing: purging every trace of Ron's presence last night and this afternoon.

I worked all day, interrupted by phone calls from him that sent me into teeth-clenching fury. He was patient and understanding, anxious to be the Considerate Male in the face of his little woman's PMS upsets. I was afraid if I saw him again I'd try to kill him.

As I worked, the litany churned in my head: *There's got to be some explanation for last night. That new date rape drug? I can't see Ron, the Mr. Clean of the South, doing that — and his astonished reaction didn't fit. Besides, it wasn't Ron who triggered this madness — it was Trevor Elliot. (Smoky bar. . .) But how do I know that? And what good would it do Elliot to put that drug in my drink? He certainly didn't benefit from it. Or did he? Is he some kind of demon, like in that movie I saw last week? Is he controlling my actions somehow? Could he make me kill Ron? He seemed to be inside my head when we were staring at each other at the party — but I think he was as surprised as I was — or was that a good act, while he did something to my mind? What triggered my attack on Ron? I've heard of demon possession — is this what it feels like? (Warm honey . . .) I wonder if I should see an exorcist. . . I don't even know how to find one; I doubt they're listed in the Yellow Pages. . . Maybe I should go back to Dr. Silverstein for a few sessions; he helped me a lot after the divorce. . . maybe I'm just too tired. . . maybe it really is PMS, but it's the wrong time of the month — or is it? I've lost track . . . maybe there's emotional stuff that I never got around to discussing with Silverstein . . . I could certainly use a vacation, but I can't leave the business . . . LuAnne's good, but she could never handle it alone. Besides, I couldn't afford a vacation; all my money's tied up in Country Cuzzin . . .There's no insanity in my family that I know of — but then I don't know enough to judge whether I'm going crazy or just under a lot of stress . . . I wonder if Dr. Silverstein's still in the area; he was talking about moving. . . (Alto sax. . .) I've got to do something!*

When Ron called again, I told him I was very tired and was going to bed early. He was considerate and understanding; I wanted to shriek at him to leave me alone. In my newly-sterilized bathroom, I took a long, hot shower. I guess I had exhausted myself, because there were no dreams that night.

🙾 🙿

Over the next few days, the horror began to dissipate somewhat. Ron, out of town on business and obviously worried, called me every evening, no matter where he was. He had an endless capacity for patience and understanding, which irritated me — I would have had more respect for him if he'd told me off. *He's really a very nice guy — I should be delighted he cares for me — but the very sound of his voice enrages me.* And the irony of my attitude was not lost on me: only a few days ago I had happily dreamed of becoming Mrs. Ronald McIntyre.

My mood swings were scary even to me, for the slightest irritation sent me into teeth-grinding fury, often followed by tears. My conversation with Trevor had lasted less than five minutes, but I couldn't get him out of my mind. I would see him on a crowded street and start toward him, only to realize it was a man who looked nothing like him. Once on the phone I thought I recognized his voice; the guy selling light bulbs (magazine subscriptions?) must have thought I was crazy, for my initial reaction was delight, then anger as I slammed the receiver down. I began to fantasize about making love to him. I gave myself stern lectures about thinking such thoughts about a married man — only to drift off into fantasy land again. One day, "waking up" from one such daydream, I found I had been writing "Trevor Elliot" over and over again on my scratch pad. Guilty and ashamed, I shredded it.

Country Cuzzin was my only salvation, and I immersed myself with a kind of desperation, working late into the night. At least on the job I could wall off the demons slobbering at the gates of my psyche. We had orders to fill, shipments to make, and one of our traveling scouts had found a source of bathroom accessories which fit perfectly into the Country Cuzzin line. With my partner LuAnne handling the day-to-day routine, I devoted my time to sales and marketing, with positive results. I was making a list of employee bonuses when LuAnne told me, "Stan Bennett is on the phone."

Bennett Interiors, a nationwide chain of stores specializing in do-it-yourself interior decoration, was one of our biggest accounts.

"And to what do I owe this honor?" I said gaily. "It was good to see you at the gala, but I wish Madge had been with you."

Stan didn't bother with pleasantries: "I'm afraid I have bad news, Daphne. The corporation has declared bankruptcy."

Stunned, I couldn't think of anything to say, and he rushed to fill the gap. "We'll be liquidating everything in the next six months. I'm so sorry, Daphne. I left things too late; I should have made changes earlier."

"You're not even going to attempt reorganization?"

"There's nothing to reorganize. The economic climate is awful right now, as you well know, and we've lost a lot of business to the home-improvement chains, and

. . . well, just between us, I made some bad investments. I've lost everything." His voice wavered.

"How is Madge taking this?" I asked.

"Better than I expected. She's a tough lady; she'll pull through."

"And what about you?"

"Right now I'm still numb. It happened so fast. . ."

"I didn't even know you were in trouble, Stan. I'm so sorry."

"We've been having cash flow problems, but the CFO went behind my back to the board and convinced them there was no hope."

"Sounds like a personal vendetta," I commented.

"I wondered the same thing, but he wouldn't talk about it. By the time I knew what was happening, the decision had been made and voted on."

"You mean you weren't even notified by your own board?"

"Oh, sure I was," he replied bitterly, "about an hour before they held the meeting. I had no time to prepare, no advance notice. It took about fifteen minutes and they voted to declare bankruptcy."

"Stan, I don't know much about publicly-traded corporations, but that doesn't sound legal! I'd suggest you get a good corporate lawyer."

There was a long pause. "You know what, Daphne? I don't give a damn. Suddenly I'm tired. I worked my ass off for this company, brought it up from a one-store mom and pop business to a nationwide chain. All I have left is my car." He chuckled raggedly. "And I'm not sure how long I'll be able to keep that."

He hesitated, sighing. "I guess you know this means we have to cancel all our outstanding orders with you. We're closing stores as fast as we can, selling stuff at fire-sale prices. We'll try to pay as much as we can on our account, but — god I hate this! — I can't make any firm commitments. I suspect we'll be paying something like twenty-five or fifty cents on the dollar, but I can't even guarantee that."

"I understand." I felt sudden pressure in my temples; my brain buzzed. There was another long pause as I tried to assimilate Stan's news.

Finally I managed, "What will you do?"

"I don't know yet. I haven't had time to think. I'll be on the phone most of the day. I want to contact the most important people personally." He sighed again, a deep, heavy sound. "I'm truly sorry, Daphne."

"I'm sorry, too, Stan, but please don't think I hold this against you. If there's any way I can help, let me know."

"Thanks. That means a lot. Take care."

"You too."

I crumpled up my list of bonuses and threw it in the trash, staring blindly out the window. Bennett Interiors represented about 75% of our revenue. Based on their last order, which had been sizeable, I had placed some large orders myself, and doubted I could cancel enough of them to make it worthwhile. Many of my suppliers were very small businesses; most were individuals, working out of their homes, sometimes part-time after their regular day jobs. Several were located in Latin America and Mexico, and those were the ones I worried about most, for the merchandise they created for me was their only source of income. José Sánchez in Bolivia fed an extended family of eight or ten on what he sold through me. If I could arrange some sort of business deal with Sylvia Elliot, Country Cuzzin might have a chance — but I had already learned the truth of the old cliché, and had no intention of counting those particular chickens until the contract was signed and the down payment had cleared the bank.

Feeling like a traitor, I pulled up my contacts list on my computer and picked up the phone.

3

The next few weeks were a blur of confusion and disappointment. Two other accounts, somehow linked with Bennett Interiors, cancelled pending orders. Sylvia Elliot called to say her developer was having temporary financial problems and wouldn't be making any decisions for a while. I wasn't particularly surprised, and I like to think I hid my disappointment well. I watched my cash flow dwindle from a comfortable stream to a trickle. Reluctantly, LuAnne and I let our part-time workers go and took over the packaging and shipping ourselves. At least there were few other expenses. We worked out of a couple bedrooms in my home, which, along with the car, had been a consolation prize of my divorce.

In the confusion, Trevor Elliot faded to a dim memory. Ron, local executive of his family's fast-growing international travel agency, was frequently — blessedly — out of the country on business. I could not understand why he was still obviously looking forward to our marriage, but he wisely didn't press me, and I took the coward's way out and kept postponing the inevitable.

At the dentist's office for a routine checkup, I thumbed listlessly through a six-month-old news magazine, wondering if I should write a check for the dental work or put it on one of the credit cards that wasn't maxed out yet. I was halfway through an article about civil problems in some obscure country in Africa before I noticed the text and photos were by Trevor West Elliot. It took me a moment to figure out why the name sounded familiar — a measure, perhaps, of how much I had recovered. He was a good writer and photographer, his text sparse and direct, his photography powerful. One picture haunted me: two small children — they looked like twins — stared with huge, dark, sad eyes into the camera, their arms protectively around one another. The caption said they hadn't survived the fighting.

I wondered how Sylvia handled his being away on assignment for so long — and I wondered again what had happened to me the night I met him. But then the hygienist called my name and I forgot about Trevor West Elliot.

The forgetting, I discovered, was temporary.

I stared out the bedroom window at the cotton fields that stretched as far as I could see, empty in the sodden Georgia afternoon. Lordy, it was hot! Perspiration trickled down my back, but I was already stripped down to my chemise and I knew Dib would have a fit if I went any further. She was a dear old thing, my black nanny, but she could be a real termagant when it came to proprieties.

I sighed, repinned a strand of hair that was plastered to the back of my neck, and turned to the bed where my husband Darcy lay, barely conscious, watching me through half-closed eyes. He raised his hand weakly and I took it in mine. Even in his hand, I could feel the dry heat of the fever that simply would not break.

"I'd ask how you're feeling, dearest one, but I think I know," I said softly.

"I'm such a burden to you, my love."

"Not at all," I smiled. "At least I have you to myself, and not on a battlefield somewhere trying to get shot."

"I already did that," he joked feebly. "I don't see any reason to try it again."

"It would've been nice if you'd avoided that particular bullet."

"I did my best."

"I know, darling. Can you sleep for a while?"

"It's so hot!"

"I'll get one of the houseboys to fan you. Would that help?"

"I'd rather you'd just sit here beside me." He hesitated. "Would you let me see your breasts?"

"What?"

"You're so beautiful, and I haven't seen you naked for so long. I'd like to look, even if I can't do anything about it. . ."

I turned away so he couldn't see my tears and began to untie my chemise.

Suddenly feet thundered up the stairs. Sam burst into the room without knocking, his eyes huge in his black face, his chest heaving, sweat pouring down his face. "Dey'se comin', missy! Dey'se soldiers marchin' on d'road!"

"How far?"

"Not more'n a mile. Mebbe two. Ah run de whole way. . ." He bent over, panting, trying to catch his breath.

We'd heard rumors, of course, but I didn't believe they'd be a threat, since the plantation was located well away from the main roads.

"How many?" Darcy asked.

"Lots, massa. Lots 'n' lots."

"Union soldiers?" I demanded.

"Yas'm."

Sherman!

"I don't think they'll bother us, Sam. . ."

"Yes, they will, April!" Darcy exclaimed, his face somehow paler than it was before. "Get the servants together and run for that old root cellar in the woods. You should be safe there until they pass."

"Sam, help me wrap Master Darcy in a blanket. We can carry him between us."

The unexpected strength in Darcy's voice shocked me. "No! I'll slow you down! Leave me! I'm dying anyhow."

Sam glanced from Darcy to me, agony apparent on his face. "Massa's right, missy. We ain't got time. Ifn we go now, we jes' might make it."

I turned on him in fury. "How dare you!" Sam cowered.

"April!" It was Darcy. "Go now! Get out of here!" He had never before raised his voice to me, but I was too upset to notice.

"No! I'm not leaving you! Sam, take the others and get into the woods. I am sure General Sherman won't harm a helpless woman and a dying man. Go!"

Sam hesitated only a second, then turned and clattered down the stairs, shouting for the house servants. In moments I heard the door slam and a babble of voices heading for the woods behind the house. Suddenly the huge old mansion was eerily silent.

I was surprised to see tears running down Darcy's face. "You bloody fool! Please, April — run! You might still have time. . ."

"If we live, we live together. If we die, we die together, my love. Life wouldn't be worth living without you anyhow. I promised till death do us part, remember?" I sat on the bed and took his hand in mine, trying not to think about what was to come. Exhausted, Darcy

seemed to fall into a deep sleep.

Gunfire in the distance! Darcy's eyes snapped open. "April, they won't spare you. Do you know what they do to women — especially a woman who's harboring a Confederate soldier?"

"I've heard rumors. I don't believe gentlemen would do that. Not to a wounded officer and his wife."

"Sherman's men aren't gentlemen, goddammit." He struggled for breath, then, in a dead voice said, "Go get my shotgun."

"That's a good idea! I can hold them off from upstairs!"

"With one shotgun you don't even know how to fire? Just go get it."

I hurried downstairs and grabbed the shotgun and some shells — I hoped they were the right ones — from the cabinet. But I couldn't find very many shells, and I knew they wouldn't be enough. Besides, Darcy wasn't strong enough to lift the gun, never mind fire it. It would have to be up to me.

Back in the bedroom, he showed me how to load both barrels and pull the trigger, pausing often to gather his strength. The sound of gunfire was nearer now, and I thought I could hear the tramp of hundreds of feet. I turned to the window, the shotgun so heavy I could hardly lift it.

"No, April. Turn it this way." Confused, I turned back to him. "Point it at me and pull the trigger," he explained patiently. "Then turn it on yourself."

"No!"

"You have no choice," he hissed. "I will love you forever, my dearest one, but those men will make sure we both die long, slow and painful deaths! You remember what happened to Lacey? The fact that you're white is not going to protect you! I can't stand thinking of what they'll do to your beautiful body. Please, my love — it's the only way. We'll be together, I promise you — but

you must do it now!"

Lacey, one of our household servants, had been waylaid by a group of drunken soldiers as she was on her way home late one night. A field hand found her body, brutally raped and mutilated.

Tears streamed down my face. I whispered, "As god is my witness, Darcy, I do not want to do this."

"You have no choice, my love. Believe me, it will be a kindness to us both. Kiss me, now, and pull the trigger."

Soldiers thundered up the stairs, but they were too late. Somehow I was flying free, Darcy laughing beside me, staring down at two mangled bodies lying side-by-side on a blood-soaked bed. The feeling of freedom was unbelievably exhilarating.

       ❧   ❧

I sat up with a jerk and a gasp, tears and sweat running down my face. The gunfire was closer now, and I turned in despair to Darcy — but he wasn't next to me in bed. How had he gotten up, weak as he was? And where had he gone? I turned on the light, but I was alone in a room totally unfamiliar to me. Slowly comprehension returned: I was once again safe in my twenty-first century home. The "gunfire" was some idiot setting off fireworks across the street.

"This has got to stop," I muttered. I hurried to the phone book and looked up Joseph Silverstein. No listing. Maybe he had merged his practice with another doctor. I looked under Psychiatrists in the Yellow Pages. No Dr. Silverstein. And I couldn't find his business card in my desk. A number of Silversteins were listed in the online directory, but none with his first name. I was on my own, with no one to talk to. Most of my friends were business associates and I was not about to share my mental deterioration with them.

Mulling over the two nightmares, I saw similarities.

In both dreams I was in a society at war, and in immi-
nent personal danger. Ron hadn't been in this one, but
I somehow *knew* that Darcy was Trevor Elliot. Apparently reading his article had triggered the dream; I must
have connected him with the war and terror he reported.
Again — the combination of violence and Trevor Elliot.
Shivering, I sat in the kitchen until well after dawn, trying to shake a sense of impending doom.

4

The next morning, LuAnne took one look at my face and said, "Geez, Daphne, are you okay?"

"Just didn't sleep well last night." I leafed through some invoices so I wouldn't have to meet her gaze.

"Is it Ron?"

I sighed. "That's part of it. I'm going to have to dump him, and I hate to hurt his feelings. He's really a very nice guy, but I can't stand the sight of him."

"What happened? Not long ago you told me you had been discussing marriage."

"That was before I got to know him." *And before I tried to kill him...* "He's just... I don't know. Boring."

LuAnne looked at me strangely and said nothing. She was a tall perky red-head, full of self-assurance I had never known. Life to LuAnne was simple and straight-forward. Nothing upset her, nothing scared her. I had hired her as my personal assistant several years ago, and, quickly seeing the potential in Country Cuzzin, she had wiped out her savings to invest as a minor partner. I knew that was all she had, and I had hated to break the news about Bennett, but she had simply nodded and replied, "Rough times ahead." The she had lifted her head and grinned. "But we'll get through it!"

Now, to fill the sudden silence, I changed the subject. "Is Frank going to be able to ship those wall hangings in time?"

"They went out Monday. I told you that yesterday, remember?"

"You don't have to sound so damned smug!"

Controlling her voice with visible effort, LuAnne said, "C'mon, Daphne. We may be business associates, but I'd like to think we're also friends. Something's been bugging you for several weeks now, and whatever it is, it's getting worse — and something tells me it isn't just Ron."

"It's the financial problems, too."

"That's probably part of it, but there's more. You've been snapping at everybody, including clients. If you can't talk to me, you've got to find someone to talk to or you'll explode."

"Is it that obvious?"

She rolled her eyes.

I dropped into a chair and stared out the window. "I'm telling you this in confidence, LuAnne. If it ever gets out, it could only have come from you."

"You know it's not going anywhere."

I hesitated. Where to begin? What to tell? What not to tell? "I met some guy at the Harmon gala. We didn't really even have a conversation; he said something casual to me, and when I looked at him our eyes locked. I swear I *knew* I had known him for ages, but I've never seen him before in my life. I could *feel* him inside my head, but that was the only contact I had with him that evening, except for an occasional puzzled glance across the room. We didn't speak again, and I haven't seen him or heard from him since. But his voice keeps echoing in my head, and I see mental images of smoky bars and black velvet. And I often hear an alto sax, but nobody else does."

I paused, fighting to keep my voice under control. "The night of the gala I had a bad dream. I was a Jew in Germany sometime around World War II, and a young Nazi officer was warning me and my husband that we had to flee because they were sending Jews to camps in the north. What is so weird is that I somehow *knew* that the Nazi officer was the guy at the party, and my husband in the dream was Ron — but my husband and I were in our sixties, and the Nazi was a kid in his early twenties. The guy I met at the party was about my age, dark haired, with green eyes. That Nazi was blond with icy blue eyes. But somehow they were the same person."

Tears ran down my face now, but I couldn't stop the verbal avalanche as I frantically tried to sort out what I was willing to tell and what I wasn't. "I didn't think too much about it, until I read an article in a news magazine yesterday written by the guy at the party — his name's Trevor West Elliot; I guess he's a photojournalist. Anyhow, last night I had another dream, and he was in it again — only this time we were about the same age, in our early twenties. We were on a southern plantation, and I don't think we'd been married very long. He had been wounded in the Civil War and sent home to die. Sherman's troops found us, and I . . . my husband insisted I take his shotgun and kill us both before we were captured. Oh, god, it was awful!"

LuAnne came around the desk and put her arms around me.

"I'm afraid I'm losing my mind!" I wailed. "I wake up from those dreams totally disoriented. I can't concentrate during the day! I thought I had my mood swings under control, but from what you say I don't. I've developed a hatred for Ron that I can't explain even to myself. I'm a mature woman with a business to run, but all I can think about is those dreams and that goddamned Trevor

Elliot and his voice and that saxophone! I think I see him on every street corner, and I don't even know him! He's happily married to an absolutely stunning woman, and I have no business even thinking about him — but I can't get him out of my mind."

LuAnne held me until I had myself more or less under control, then pushed a box of tissues toward me and said quietly, "You're not losing your mind, Daphne. I strongly suspect you're experiencing spontaneous past-life regressions."

I blew my nose. "The hell's that?"

"Well, we've never discussed religion or anything, but there are those who believe in reincarnation."

She hesitated, waiting for my reaction, but all I said was, "I'm listening."

"Okay. Let's assume for a moment that there is such a thing. If you've lived other lives in the past, it makes sense that you should be able to remember them. Only, during the period between lives, we agree to certain things before we enter the next life. One of the things we agree to is that we will be pretty much unable to recall any past lives."

"What's the point in having more than one life? Besides, if I recall my Sunday school lessons, the Bible says 'It is appointed unto man once to die, and after that the judgment.'"

"Well, yes — but . . . Look, I'm not sure how religious you are, and I don't want to step on your toes, but you did ask a question, and you may not be comfortable with the answer."

"Just tell me what's wrong with me. Am I going to be a cockroach in my next lifetime?"

LuAnne laughed. "Hardly."

Abruptly she stood and went to the kitchen, returning with a glass of ice water. "Drink up, kid. It'll calm you down a little." She watched me until she was sure I was settling down, then continued, "Okay. Let me try to answer your question about why, and then we'll go back to what's happening to you now. And, no, you won't come back as a bug."

She took a deep breath and sat facing me. "We are not just physical beings who think. We're spirits, temporarily inhabiting physical bodies here on this earth in order to learn certain lessons. I won't bother to go into the whys and wherefores of that now, but each lifetime we kind of 'major' in a particular lesson or two. I know, for instance, that I spent one or two lives as a religious recluse, learning how to find spiritual enlightenment in a monastic environment."

"What good does it do to learn lessons if we forget them?"

She smiled. "Good question. On some higher level of consciousness we do remember. Once we have mastered a particular lesson, we go on to another life and another lesson. Like when we were in college, we never forget that water is made up of hydrogen and oxygen, even if we can't remember what question number 16 was on the chemistry final. And what we learned when we lived in, for instance, ancient Rome will still have a subtle influence on us in this life.

"Also, memories of past lives kind of 'leak' into present ones. I'm sure you've heard of people who go to a foreign city for the first time in their lives and somehow *know* where to go and they recognize landmarks they've never seen before. It's probably also why some people learn certain foreign languages more easily than others: they no doubt spoke that language in some prior lifetime. You with me so far?"

I nodded. "Makes a lot more sense than some of the other explanations I've heard."

"One word of warning: don't assume that everything I tell you is gospel truth. I learned long ago that we each have to find our own path. Mine won't work for you and yours won't work for me. We can help each other, give each other advice and suggestions as I'm doing now — but ultimately we each have to find our own answers."

"Where did you learn all this stuff, LuAnne? I've never seen this side of you before."

"It's not something I talk about, because most people don't understand or aren't ready for the information. I've been aware almost all my life that I've lived before. For me, reincarnation was a given from early childhood, and I got into a lot of trouble with the other kids and their parents when I tried to share my beliefs." She smiled ruefully. "I got sent home from grade school several times and finally learned to keep my mouth shut — and that's as it should be. Nobody has any business imposing their belief system on another, no matter how convinced they are it's the right one. As I said, we each have to find our own path."

"So what you're saying is that I really was a Jew in Nazi Germany, and that I was also Scarlett O'Hara during the Civil War."

"Well, your name probably wasn't Scarlett O'Hara, but you got the idea."

"Why did this start happening all of a sudden?"

"I suspect you agreed, before you were born, to meet this guy — what's his name? Trevor? — at this point in your life. I'd guess you two have something — a problem or a lesson — that you agreed to work on together. Obviously there's a bond; you said you somehow recognized him, and he apparently felt the same thing."

I nodded. "I remember thinking I've *always* known him. But the thought was so stupid I brushed it aside."

"You might try listening to your intuition more," LuAnne smiled. "Personally, I think the story is fascinating."

"Well, I'll never see him again. He's very married to a beautiful and charming woman and it was just a coincidence that we were both at that gala."

LuAnne laughed. "Don't bet on it. I predict you'll

somehow run into him again. The meeting at the party was a dry run. And remember this, Daphne: there is no such thing as coincidence. You agreed to meet him again in this lifetime. This is just the first chapter."

Remembering what had happened with Ron, I muttered, "I hope you're wrong."

"Why? Aren't you curious?"

"I don't get involved with married men. Period." Then, because I was afraid if we talked any more I'd tell her what happened with Ron — and I wasn't about to tell anyone about those two ghastly incidents — I picked up some papers and escaped to my desk.

༒ ༒

Financially, things didn't get any worse over the next few weeks, but they didn't improve, either. I tried to count each small blessing, but it got harder to get up in the morning and face another day of demanding creditors, angry suppliers, and empty order forms. My conversation with the loan officer at the bank didn't help. "I'm sorry, Ms. Morris, but you simply don't have the assets. There is no inventory to speak of, and your ex-husband's name is still on the mortgage for the house. I'm afraid you don't have the legal right to place a second mortgage on it, not without his signature — and the bank probably wouldn't give you one anyhow, considering the economic climate right now. I can possibly loan you $5,000 on your signature alone, but I can't go any higher than that."

"I need at least twenty." *I really need thirty. . .*

"I'd like to help. Really. Unfortunately, my hands are tied."

I thought I detected smug satisfaction in his piggy little eyes, but there was no point in arguing.

The story was pretty much the same at two other lending institutions.

"Banks just aren't lending to businesses or individuals — even those with excellent credit and assets," one of them told me.

"Why?"

"It has to do with the new reserves requirements — actually any type of lending issues. Right now nobody knows for sure what's going to happen, and all lending institutions are walking on eggs." He shifted uncomfortably in his big expensive leather chair. "Perhaps you could get a loan from family members. Or you might try those new crowdsourcing websites. I understand some startups have had great success with them. Or maybe your ex-husband could lend a hand."

I didn't even want to think about that. Fortunately, the divorce had been fairly amicable, which was why his name remained on the mortgage; he had generously offered to do that in case I couldn't meet the monthly payments. But I had paid a high price for my independence, and until now I had been doing very well financially. I wasn't about to crawl back to him with my begging bowl.

Ron still called me nearly every evening, and I had been careful not to mention my troubles to him, but one evening he could tell I had been crying and begged me to let him share the burden. Scared and vulnerable, I sobbed out the whole story of Bennett's bankruptcy and its domino effect.

Making little noises of sympathy, Ron listened until I ran out of breath. "Maybe there's another answer, darling." I felt a flash of irritation at his possessive little term of affection.

"I've tried everything and I haven't been able to come up with any other answers," I answered. The thought crossed my mind that maybe God was causing my financial problems as some kind of punishment for what I'd done to Ron.

"I have some news," he continued. "I've been promoted to president of the corporate sales division."

"How nice for you, Ron," I mumbled. "Congratulations."

He hesitated. "It will mean my moving back to corporate headquarters in Miami."

"Oh."

"Is that all? Just 'oh'?"

"Uh, well — I mean, I'm delighted for you. I know you like Miami."

"Daphne — I want you to come with me."

"What? Oh, I don't see how I could, not with things as they are now financially."

"Maybe it's time you accepted the fact that Country Cuzzin isn't going to make it. Maybe it's time to look in a different direction."

"I've spent ten years building this business! I'm not going to abandon it now!"

"No, of course not," he backpedaled hastily. "That's not what I meant. What I was thinking was that we could get married, and move to Miami, and start Country Cuzzin again there. You'd be somewhat closer to your Latin American suppliers, and we could rent a warehouse so you could keep an inventory instead of having your suppliers direct-ship. That way you could buy in larger quantities and be able to ship to customers the same day."

"And where am I going to get the money for that? I'd have to buy LuAnne out and we're not meeting expenses now."

"Well, I. . ." He sighed. "I know you value your independence, and I certainly wouldn't want to take that away from you. But if we incorporated in Florida and went into this as partners, I could help financially. And maybe having a man on board would help you get further financing. Especially if you were married to him. . . I know it's not politically correct to say this these days, but let's face facts: women have made real progress in shattering the glass ceiling, but it's still there. I'd remain a minor stockholder, of course," he added quickly, "and that would work to our advantage, because then it would still be a minority corporation — owned by a woman."

"You're still willing to do that after . . . after what happened?"

"Of course — only I'd really like you to see a therapist of some sort. You know, try to find out what caused it. I know some women are especially violent during the PMS period, but you've never displayed that kind of aggression before. Let's hope it was only a fluke — maybe it was some sort of chemical reaction or something. But I know a few excellent psychiatrists in Miami who could be of real help."

"I don't know. I need to think about it."

"Sure! I don't want to push you into anything, but maybe you could fly down for a week or something, get to know my family, check out warehouses in the area, that kind of thing."

"What if I get violent again?"

There was a long pause. "I hope we can find answers to that, darling."

I wanted to tell him to leave me the hell alone, but his offer was tempting — and I was still dealing with overwhelming guilt about my attack. Guilt and fear. Ron was a truly nice guy — maybe a bit too nice — and I should have been ecstatic over his willingness to continue our relationship. Only I was beginning to suspect I couldn't live with him for the rest of my life, and I was afraid I might try to kill him again if he irritated me enough. I had one failed marriage on my record; I didn't want the second one to end in murder.

I sighed. "Let me think about it. I'm not capable of thinking clearly right now."

"I'll call you tomorrow. Sleep well, my dear."

I gritted my teeth. "Good night."

But maybe this was the beginning of a change of direction in my life.

5

Or maybe not.

❧   ❦

"Raus! Raus! Raus! Raus!"

I was cold — numb with cold. My feet were useless blobs of ice, and I couldn't stop coughing. It was still dark, but the blare of the loudspeaker would not be denied. "Raus! Raus! Stehen sie auf! Raus!" *The woman next to me on the plank we used for a bed shoved me roughly off the edge.* "Get out of my way, you stupid bitch! I'm not going to miss roll-call because of a lazy slut!"

Roll-call seemed to last forever. I swayed and the woman next to me caught me just before I fell, whispering, "Hold on, Deborah" *— but the guards saw it and dragged us both out of line. I was too tired to fight; I collapsed on the frozen ground. I knew what was coming and it was a relief.*

Sometimes I had tried to remember what life was like before we were arrested and brought to this hid-

eous camp. Warm food? Warm clothes? They were vague memories, and I wondered if they had ever been real. I felt as if I'd been here all my life — and I knew there was no hope for me. None but death, and now I looked forward to that.

I thought of Mordecai — my dearly beloved husband — the cause of all of this. And where is he now? *I wondered bitterly.* He put us here. I hope he's suffering more than I am! He never listened to me.

"I have a respected position at the university," he had assured me. "God will protect us. He has always looked out for His people, and He won't fail us now."

So this is how my dear husband protects me and God looks out for us, *I thought angrily.* If we had listened to Kurt, we could have escaped! If we had paid attention to the disappearances in the neighborhood, we could have gotten out in time! But, no, Mordecai had to play Rabbi Full of Wisdom, faithful anointed of God!

Rough hands — the hands of my own people — stripped me naked and dragged me toward the ovens. By the time they turned the gas on, I was unconscious from the cold. My last thought was, this is all Mordecai's fault.

❧   ❧

I awoke with a raging headache and a sore throat. But now, at least, I understood some of my deep-seated anger at Ron. I had never been able to forgive him in his incarnation as Mordecai, and apparently I had died still vilifying him.

Even in this lifetime I couldn't let go of my hatred.

I kept putting Ron off, torn between the rescue he offered me and the growing realization that marriage to him would be a disaster.

❧   ❧

A few days later, LuAnne told me, "There's a Sylvia Elliot on the phone. She says you met at Harmon's party. . ."

I grabbed the phone before the name Elliot could register with LuAnne. "Hello, Sylvia! How are you?"

"I'm fine — and I've got great news! I showed the developer the catalog you sent me, and it's exactly what he wants. Can we get together for lunch?"

"When and where?"

"Um. . . I have to spend tomorrow with a client; she wants her drawing room redone. How about Friday? Are you free?"

"Yes."

"Do you know Fisherman's Dock on Holland Avenue?"

"Yep. Is 1:00 okay?"

"Sounds great. I'll meet you there."

Fisherman's Dock was the local yuppie wallowing pit, festooned with faux fisherman's paraphernalia — nets and lobster pots and gaffs — overlooking the barges on the river. The waiters, dressed like scruffy sailors, cheerfully insulted the customers. The bar, curved like a boat hull and stretching the length of the room, was staffed by bartenders who boasted there wasn't a cocktail they couldn't make. One unshaven pirate, wearing an eye patch and a bandana, was juggling lemons and eggs when Sylvia, dressed in a tasteful grey business suit and looking as if she'd just come from a beauty salon, came through the door. She greeted me with a grin. "I feel like celebrating," she said. "Join me in a glass of champagne?"

"Do you think we'll both fit?"

She groaned. "That is so *old!*"

"Sorry. It's the best I could do. What are we celebrating?"

"I've signed a contract with our developer, and I'm going to need Country Cuzzin very soon."

"I hope it's not too late," I replied, trying to keep my voice light. The maître d' led us to a table, handed us menus, murmured our waiter's name, took our order for champagne, and disappeared.

"Why too late?" Sylvia asked.

Briefly, I recounted the last few months. "It's been a road straight through hell. I'm not sure we can pull it out."

She studied me carefully. "Would you be willing to accept some sort of partnership with our firm? I'd have to check with my partners and board of directors, of course, but we can at least discuss it."

Elliot & Dayle Interiors was nowhere near as large as Bennett — I'd done some research since I'd last talked to Sylvia — but they were a solid firm that specialized in upscale offices and manors like the ones in Riverside Park.

"I'd certainly be willing to explore the idea — and I'd want to clear it with my partner. But can Elliot & Dayle buy in the volume I'd need to get me out of this mess?"

"I would think, with LakePointe, that there would be quite a lot of merchandise changing hands. And we'll be bidding for similar contracts; we've decided to expand our horizons beyond the prestige homes and offices. Maybe we can help with some short-term financing, too, but that's not official; I'll need to check with the board."

We talked and speculated for the rest of the afternoon while the luncheon crowd dissipated, leaving us alone in the dining room, an empty champagne bottle between us. Sylvia's quirky sense of humor and straightforward attitude appealed to me, and it didn't take us long to realize we had a lot in common. Suddenly my cell phone beeped. "Oh, I forgot to turn the stupid thing off," I exclaimed. "I know this is bad manners, but would you mind if I took this call? It's my partner LuAnne."

"Go ahead. It's probably a new client begging for a million dollars' worth of merchandise — cash on delivery," she said with a grin.

"Daphne, it's LuAnne. I hate to bother you, but Ron's called several times from Miami, very upset because you haven't returned his calls. He wants you to call him as soon as possible."

"Did you tell him where I am?"

"No. I wasn't sure you wanted me to."

"Good. But do me a favor: the next time he calls tell him. . ." I hesitated. I didn't have the right to involve LuAnne in my personal problems. "Just tell him you haven't been able to reach me."

"You sure about this?"

"I hope so."

"Okay."

Sylvia smiled as I disconnected the call. "A client?"

"No a . . . uh . . . friend . . . former friend. . ."

Sylvia eyed me for a moment. "I know it's none of my business, but are you attached to anyone?"

"Not really. There is — or was — a guy — only he's about to move back to Miami, and I can't find it in myself to be upset about it. I suppose I should be, but the only emotion I can muster is relief."

"Oh, wow, sounds like the romance of the century," she chuckled. "Was that the guy you were with at the gala?"

"Mmm. He's nice enough, really — and very much in love with me, from what he says. I just . . . I don't know, Sylvia; it's hard to put into words. It sounds so awful, but the truth is he's boring and somehow everything he says infuriates me."

She grinned. "I know exactly what you mean. After you've discussed the weather, the football game, and what's on TV, there's not much left. And so many men are intimidated by intelligent women."

I nodded ruefully, but I wasn't about to tell her the whole story. "As far as I can tell, he has no interests outside the travel agency he works for — which his family owns. He's been promoted — president of one of their divisions, if I recall — and I guess, in his own field, hc's very competent. But I get the impression he thinks my business is a cute little thing for his little darling to put-ter at, but it's not anywhere near as important as an in-ternational travel agency."

"Oh, god, Daphne, dump him!"

"I tried to, but apparently he's not convinced; Lu-Anne says he's called several times — and I guess I'm having second thoughts. I'm not sure Country Cuzzin can survive — and he offered to help finance the busi-ness and set me up in Miami with a warehouse so I could keep an inventory."

Sylvia reached across the table, imprisoned my wrist, and skewered me with her blazing eyes. I was startled to realize they were as green as Trevor's. "You listen to me, Daphne Morris. You are an intelligent, independent woman with one hell of a lot of business savvy and an excellent market for your stuff. Don't you ever, *ever* sell yourself to a man! You can make it on your own, and don't *ever* let anybody tell you otherwise!"

Stunned by her ferocity, I simply stared at her. She grinned sheepishly and released my wrist. "Sorry. I get on my soapbox sometimes, but I really mean it. Sure, there will be some rough times, but remember there's truth in the old saying that adversity makes for strong character. My brother was certainly impressed with you, and he's a pretty good judge of people. That's one of the reasons I spoke to you that night. I figured if my jaded brother could be bowled over by a woman, she must be pretty special."

Something short-circuited in my brain. "Your broth-er?"

"At the gala, remember?"

"That was your brother? I thought you two were married."

She threw back her head and laughed, reminding me

of Trevor's easy laughter that night. They were so much alike — why hadn't I seen it before?

"Actually, people often think that, and I admit we sometimes play on it. The truth is we're twins. I love my brother dearly, and he's one reason my marriage broke up. Trevor and I are very close, and my husband was jealous."

"I can see why. It's obvious you're very fond of each other."

She nodded. "But we're both very independent. There were other reasons that marriage broke up — Trevor was not in any way to blame. But he was so kind and gentle when it did. He's a good man, is my weird globe-trotting brother."

I waited, hoping she'd say more, determined not to reveal how interested I was. Finally, keeping my voice as casual as possible, I asked, "What does he do?"

"He's a freelance photojournalist. A good one, they tell me. Frankly, I don't know much about it, except that he's gone for weeks at a time, comes home exhausted looking — and sometimes smelling — as if he's been sleeping under bridges, sleeps the clock around, then holes up and works on his computer until the article is finished. He's like a hermit, muttering to himself, drinking endless cups of coffee, impossible to communicate with. Then, once the assignment is on the way to the editor, he undergoes some sort of transformation and suddenly he's the charming party boy you met at the gala. And he can be so sweet and funny. . . Sort of a likeable Jekyll and Hyde."

"You're obviously very fond of him." *Shut up, Daphne — you're repeating yourself!*

"Trevor and I kind of brought each other up. Our parents were killed in an airplane crash when we were six. Our grandparents raised us, and they were good people, but very strict. We've been close all our lives, as twins often are, and that brought us closer." She grinned.

"Between you and me, there are times when I wish he *weren't* my brother. He's an awfully hard act to follow, but my current guy seems to understand and he's quite comfortable with Trevor, thank god."

"I can see that could be a problem."

She nodded. "Trevor's fondness for his twin, his constant traveling, and his weird ways when he's working, don't make particularly good ingredients for a long-lasting relationship for him, either. He was married once, but it only lasted about a year."

I didn't dare ask the next question, hoping she'd offer the information. Instead, much to my disappointment, she changed the subject.

"Which brings up another matter," she said, suddenly brisk. "You always manage to show up just when I need you."

She grinned at the blank expression on my face.

"Trevor is due home this week, and next week — he's promised me he'll have the assignment completed by then — I'm having a small dinner party for a few friends. I need another woman to complete the set; would you be available on Saturday evening next week? It won't be anything fancy — probably drinks at 7:00 and dinner at 8:00 at my place."

"Um. . . I think I'm free." Feeling like the phony I was, I made a show of checking my calendar. "Yes, I can make it. I'd love to."

"You sure? You sound kind of doubtful."

"I didn't mean to. You just caught me by surprise. One minute you're lecturing me and the next you're inviting me to dinner."

"I'm sorry! I do get intense sometimes, I know. I hope I didn't offend you."

It was my turn to grin. "Not at all. It's refreshing, actually, to talk to someone who speaks honestly and isn't working on some private agenda. Give me a little time; I'll get used to it."

Suddenly life looked a whole lot brighter, and it wasn't just the champagne.

Then I remembered LuAnne's prediction.

6

In spite of what I'd told Sylvia, I wasn't at all sure I wanted to be a part of her little dinner party. I had no idea how Trevor would feel about me, or how I'd react to him. I couldn't dissociate our weird exchange at the gala with my suddenly violent behavior — and it seemed every time I encountered Trevor, even if it was only via a news magazine, I had nightmares.

In addition, the memory of my rage at Ron haunted me, and understanding its basis didn't help a bit because I wasn't certain whether it was directed only at Ron or at any male I might become attached to. I envisioned taking one look at Trevor and attacking him — or running screaming into the street, hacking some passing stranger to death.

Grimly I struggled to replace that mental image with one of my greeting him calmly and coolly, then ignoring him the rest of the evening, leaving him to wrestle with his own confusion and disappointment.

Needing something to prop up my faltering courage, I spent more than I should have on a simple little "basic black" evening dress that set off my dark eyes and hair and hid the ten pounds I hadn't bothered to lose. Pearl earrings and a matching single-strand necklace were the only jewelry I would wear.

I decided not to mention the invitation to LuAnne. Although her theory was better than thinking I was going mad, I wasn't convinced, and I didn't want to give her an opportunity to say I told you so.

Friday night I went to bed early, hoping for a good night's sleep. It was not to be.

❧   ☙

"You won't have much time," my trainer told me as he wrapped my wrists with leather straps. "Is that too tight?"

I shook my head.

"Antonius is good — very good," Gaius continued. "He's been trained in the best gladiator schools in the country, and there's a lot of money on him. If you let him get the upper hand, he'll kill you. He stands half a head taller than you, and he's strong, but he tires easily, so he'll try to move in fast for a quick kill. Your quickness can win this for you. Stay out of reach and keep him moving. When he begins to tire, strike quickly — and none of your clowning."

I nodded; I'd heard all this before, but I knew Gaius needed to talk out his nervousness. "Win this one, and you'll win yourself more than your freedom," he went on. "The emperor has already told me he has his eye on you, so don't disappoint me." He clapped me on the shoulder. "Fight well, Marcus. You're a good man and the emperor will have my own head if I lose you."

I checked my armor, retied my sandals, and bowed low before the small altar Gaius had allowed me to keep in my cell. "O, divine Goddess," I whispered, "be with me this day. Give my hands strength, my feet swiftness, my heart courage. You alone have brought me this far, and all my victories have been thanks to you. Don't fail me now, my beloved Goddess. To you alone the glory. Grant me your power and your victory, not only for myself but for the woman I love."

I felt a gentle explosion near my heart, and I knew she — warrior Goddess with a sword for a tongue, she of the strong arm, the warrior's hope — I knew she would not fail me this day. I thought of Myrah, my lady of the laughing green eyes, and a smile rose to my lips. Was ever man so blessed by the love of such a woman? Though she, too, was a slave, Gaius had promised she would be mine if I won today. I rose and strode into the arena, my spirits high. I would win this one — I had no doubt. I would win for Myrah and Gaius and my Goddess.

The trumpets sounded; the crowd spotted me and roared. Excitement raced through me. Slave I might be, but they loved me, and I would give them a good fight and a memorable victory.

The emperor had decreed that this battle would be with swords and knives only. No baby toys like nets and spears that kept a man at a distance from his enemy. This would be close combat — my specialty. I grinned and saluted the emperor, then the crowd, which roared again.

The trumpets sounded again and behind me my opponent Antonius bowed. I heard hisses and boos from the audience — but there were a few cheers, also, quickly hushed. "Are you prepared to die, coward?" Antonius muttered to me. "Concede now and live or I will spill your guts upon the sand this day."

"I smell a foul fart — is it from your mouth? Face your death with what little honor you can summon," I snarled, "for you shall die the death of a dog, as becomes your station." I laughed as black anger suffused his face. All to the good — his anger would make him

*foolish. "Why did they send me a woman to spar with?"
I taunted. "Are you the best they could find? I'm insulted!"*

*He swung his sword and I sprang out of his way
just in time. I could feel the power in his swing, the
wind of its passing on my cheek. If it had connected, I
would even now be spilling my life upon the hot sand.
But Antonius had misjudged my speed, and I was safe.
Out of reach, I flashed him a rude gesture and disdain-
fully turned my back on him, deliberately goading him.
I heard his roar — followed by the crowd's roar — as he
came for me.*

*I sidestepped and spun at the last minute, swat-
ting his ass with the flat of my sword as he passed. The
crowd roared its glee, and suddenly I knew I could win.
His size and strength had won him many battles, but it
quickly became apparent to me that he wasn't good at
anticipating the unexpected; he was a rule-follower. So
I toyed with him, to the crowd's delight.*

*I pretended to be dancing, my arms around my
sword as if it were a woman, my face rapt. Sometimes
the dance got rather energetic as I danced out of reach,
but always I managed to stay ahead of him, leading
him a merry chase back and forth across the arena.
Once his sword nicked my ear (Goddess, that was
close!), and I raced across the arena to the emperor's
box, miming extreme distress at the wound.*

*Torn between amusement and suspicion that his
champion was a coward, the emperor imperiously
motioned me back to the center of the arena. I walked
slowly, reluctantly, head down, the picture of dejection.
But Gaius was right — my clowning was a mistake; I
had given my enemy time to breathe.*

*With a roar, he came at me, and this time I couldn't
get away from him. Our swords clashed, and for the
first time I felt fear. His strokes were powerful and he
had a longer reach — at close quarters he was vicious.*

I was on the defensive, backing across the arena. The crowd was silent, caught up in the drama, the only sound the ring of our swords and our labored breathing. As he backed me to the wall, I knew I was seconds from death.

Suddenly a woman screamed, "Antonius!" a high, hysterical shriek that shattered the silence and jangled to the marrow of my bones. It seemed to come from directly behind him. Startled, he hesitated and glanced over his shoulder. It was all I needed.

I tripped him, sending him sprawling, and hacked at his sword arm. His sword went flying, blood gushing from a severed artery. He reached for his knife and tried to scramble after his sword at the same time, but I gave him no chance, slicing again and again, pounding at him until he subsided, obviously addled and bleeding profusely. I put my foot on his throat and shoved him back to the ground, my sword point digging into his remaining good arm. Then I glanced at the emperor, who was watching with open-mouthed delight. The crowd roared for blood. I raised my sword above my head and looked to the emperor for the signal. Laughing, he turned two thumbs down. The crowd went wild as I hacked at Antonius' neck and held the head up by the hair, my foot planted firmly on his chest. Someone had told me that there is life and comprehension for a few seconds after a head is severed from the body. I smiled into the vacantly staring eyes of my enemy. "See?" I quipped. "No more than a smelly fart — signifying nothing." Then I spat in his face and hurled the head into the stands, turning in disgust from the mad scramble for it.

Gaius met me at the gate, his eyes almost lost in his grin. "Well done, my man! Well done!"

"I owe that woman my thanks," I replied. "I don't know whether I could have gotten out of that corner if she hadn't screamed."

"What woman?"

"The woman who screamed his name, making him hesitate just long enough for me to trip him. You must have heard it — the arena was completely silent except for her scream."

Gaius studied me with narrowed eyes. "I heard no scream — nor did anyone else, I'll wager, or they would have mentioned it. You were imagining things."

"Nay, Gaius. Antonius heard it, too, and glanced over his shoulder to see who was there. It seemed to come from directly behind him. It was his undoing — and it was loud enough that everyone in the arena must have heard it."

"Say nothing of this," Gaius whispered furiously, leading me toward the emperor's throne, "and keep a civil tongue in your head. This is no time for your theatrics."

I nodded and bowed to my emperor.

He studied me for several minutes while I waited in what I hoped was proper humility. "It was a close contest today," he commented.

"It was the Goddess' will that I win, my liege. I give her all the honor, for it was she who gave me the strength and courage."

"He nearly had you dead against that wall."

"I was in no real danger, as you saw."

"You are very sure of yourself."

"I have proven myself, sire, many times. And the Goddess is on my side."

"Yes," he conceded, "there is that." He pondered for a moment, then turned to my trainer. "Gaius Andronicus, this man is yours?"

"He is, my lord," Gaius murmured bowing low. "I trained him myself."

"You did well."

"Thank you, my liege," Gaius bowed even lower.

"I do not want him wasted in the arena. I have plans

for him. Will you release him to me?"

"It would be an honor, sire. He is a good man, and trustworthy. I hate to lose him, of course — but he deserves better than to die in the arena, and I know he will serve his emperor with honor."

"Send him to me in the morning. I'm placing him in command of my palace guard."

I gasped in astonishment and dropped to my knees. "Such an honor, my lord and my emperor! How can I thank you?"

He smiled wryly. "By ridding my palace of those who plot my death."

"I will hound them to the ends of the earth!"

"Just get rid of them. I don't care how you do it." He waved his hand and the interview was over.

That evening Myrah came to my room, eyes brimming with love and pride. I took her in my arms, cherishing the feel of her, the smell of her. I buried my face in her hair and we clung to each other. "I am to go with you, Marcus," she murmured, her green eyes wide with wonder. "That is, if you'll have me. . ." she teased.

"Wherever I go from now on, my beloved, you will be with me. This was ordained from the beginning. I know now the Goddess loves us both, and we have a great work to do together."

☨ ☩

I awoke with a gasp, my heart pounding. But this time I wasn't as disoriented, thanks to LuAnne, and I sat cross-legged in the middle of my bed, mulling over what I'd experienced. Another past life? But this one had a surprising twist. I was a man in this one — and Trevor, somehow, was the woman Myrah. Was that possible?

Strangely enough, I drifted back to sleep and slept well the rest of the night.

The next morning I called LuAnne as early as I dared.

"LuAnne, it's Daphne. Have you got a few minutes?"

"Sure. You okay?"

"I'm not sure."

"What's up?"

"I had another dream last night." I wasn't ready to tell her about the concentration camp dream.

She chuckled. "Lemme get my coffee." A few seconds later, "Okay. Talk."

After I recounted the gladiator dream, I asked, "How could I possibly have been a man?"

"Not only possible, it's probable. We explore physical life as both sexes, and as both 'good' people and 'bad' people. I was a male interrogator during the Spanish Inquisition. Not a life I'm proud of. But the idea is to investigate the whole spectrum of experience. I'm sure you were a man in many other reincarnations. And, from what you've told me, I think you kind of specialize in violent lives."

"Is that bad?"

"Neither good or bad. It just *is*. Apparently you feel there's something you can learn from them."

I thought of my last, disastrous evening with Ron. "Is it possible I'm attracted to, or prone to, violence?"

"Yup."

I groaned. "I really wanted to hear that."

LuAnne laughed. "Maybe in this life you've agreed to break that habit — learn a new way of living, without the violence. We've never talked about your childhood — it wasn't unhappy, was it?"

"Quite the contrary. It was almost boringly happy. My biggest trauma was getting stung by a bee when I was four."

"So maybe in this lifetime you've agreed to explore happiness and non-violence."

"Then why does Trevor Elliot trigger such vio —" I caught myself on the verge of mentioning the two ugly scenes with Ron — "such violent dreams?"

"I don't have all the answers. Maybe they're not-so-subtle reminders that you have some karmic debt to pay."

"Some what?"

"Karmic debt. Kind of an ongoing debit and credit sheet. Trevor earned some karmic credit when he tried to warn you in the World War II life, although that may have been wiped out by what he was doing otherwise as a Nazi. You earned yourself some karmic debt when you killed that gladiator, and you may have to make that up to him in another life, if you haven't already."

"How the hell are we supposed to keep track?" *And how much karmic debt did I pile up with Ron?*

"I'm not sure. But from what I can tell, on a spiritual level you know, and you will be given opportunities to repay it. It can be repaid in other ways, though, by doing some good for someone else. Helping little old ladies across the street, that kind of thing. Did you recognize the other gladiator as someone you know in this lifetime?"

"No. No connection I can see."

I was trying to assimilate all this when LuAnne said, "The other times you've had these regressions — dreams — they've been triggered by seeing Trevor or reading something by him. Any idea what triggered this one?"

I sighed. "I wasn't going to tell you this, but I'll be seeing him tonight."

"What? How?"

"Remember Sylvia Elliot who called a week or so ago?"

"Of Elliot & Dayle? The ones we're — omigod!"

"Yes. She's his sister, not his wife. She invited me to a small dinner party she's giving tonight." Suddenly I was close to tears. "And I'm scared to death!"

"Why?"

"I don't know what this guy does to me! He triggers some kind of insanity in me! I'm afraid I'll do something

stupid! The last time I met him I turned into a. . . a demon!" *And yet I can't stay away from him. . . Black velvet and bourbon. . .*

"Hey, calm down! They were just dreams, Daphne.
They can't harm you."

You don't know about that fiasco with Ron. "I wish
I believed you. . . LuAnne, is it possible to be possessed
by demons?"

"Like in the movies? Well, in theory, yeah, it's possible — but not anywhere near as likely as they make it
sound. You have to be willing — open the door for the
demon, so to speak. Don't worry — you're not demon
possessed."

"How do you know?"

"Trust me. And you're not gonna do anything stupid
tonight. You'll go, you'll have a nice evening, you'll come
home. End of story."

"It's not and you know it."

"You can blow this all out of proportion if you want
to, but I'd advise against it. You'll be fine. Don't drink too
much, and keep your wits about you. One reason that
first encounter was so devastating was that you weren't
prepared for it. Now you are. You know what being with
him can do, so put up your walls and keep your distance."

"You make it sound so easy."

"It will be. You'll see. You'll come home wondering
what you were so worried about." She laughed. "But call
me tomorrow and let me know how it went."

"I may show up on your doorstep tonight in hyster-
ics."

"I'll be here. But I don't think you will. C'mon, Daphne. Put on that all-business persona I've seen you do so
well, and have a pleasant evening with a very, *very* old
friend." She laughed at her own joke. "I kind of wish I
could be a mouse in your pocket."

"You could go in my place. . ."

"Not a chance. Have fun and call me in the morning."

7

If I had subconscious fantasies of Trevor sweeping me off my feet in front of the startled guests, I was disappointed. He shook my hand warmly — without kissing it — and avoided my eyes. For the first time it occurred to me that our last encounter may not have had the same impact on him as it did on me. Or was he, like me, stunned and frightened by it? A little put off by his apparent indifference, I was also relieved, because it enabled me to maintain what LuAnne called my all-business persona. At least I wasn't in danger of killing anybody. Yet.

Another woman, whom Sylvia introduced simply as "our friend Kathy", seemed to have appropriated Trevor, gazing moistly at him and hanging on his every word, although I noticed she was wearing a wedding ring. She was overdressed in a gauzy, fussy evening gown about ten years out of date, with a crinoline shawl of some sort that stood up behind her head like one of those high collars Queen Bess used to wear. Well endowed physically, she did her best to give Trevor a clear view as often as possible, and I wondered how much strain the tight bodice could take. I found it difficult to imagine Trevor being attracted to such a woman, but he was gentle and courteous with her.

My dinner partner was an accountant, balding, over-weight and middle-aged before his time, without, as far as I could tell, any sense of humor whatsoever. He seemed well educated and articulate, although he spoke with a distinct lisp. His soft pudgy hands, with long manicured nails like a woman's, gave me the creeps.

Sylvia's "guy", as she introduced him, was Vance Upshire, CEO of multi-faceted megabucks Upshire Con-struction. I liked him immediately. Tall, slim and grey-haired, his blue eyes sparkled with wisdom and humor. It was apparent that he was very fond of Sylvia, perfectly capable of keeping up with her quick wit, and not in the least intimidated by her beauty or her intelligence. "He keeps me in line," Sylvia confided to me.

I found myself wishing he weren't quite so interested in *her*.

The Lornigans, a Presbyterian minister and his wife, were well-read and open-minded. Mrs. Lornigan wore a simple blue dress that set off her flawless skin and blonde hair. Her husband, in neatly tailored pinstripe suit and conservative tie, looked like a successful invest-ment banker. He and Trevor traded wickedly inventive insults.

"You were gone so long this last time I thought you were going to stay in Timbuktu or wherever it was," Pas-tor Lornigan commented. "What happened? Tired of the primitive conditions? Or did you miss my sermons?"

"Neither. I ran out of women." Lornigan shouted with delighted laughter. Kathy scowled. I had to smile, but my companion seemed not to have heard the ex-change at all.

Once we overcame our initial reserve, the conversa-tion was far-reaching and fascinating. Trevor the globetrotter was a gifted raconteur, and it turned out that Sylvia was also widely traveled, so their observations made for a lively evening.

Inevitably, conversation turned to the current uprising in Nueva Sangria. "They can't possibly maintain it," Trevor commented. "They have neither the financing nor the manpower."

"What started it?" the pastor's wife wanted to know.

Trevor shrugged. "Who can say? Most of it is the huge gap between the proverbial haves and have-nots."

"Part of it is the pressure the United States is putting on the cocaine trade, isn't it?" Vance asked. "The drug trade is very big down there — it's common knowledge that the president of Nueva Sangria has the biggest coca plantation in the country."

"It's a difficult situation," Trevor acknowledged. "The surrounding countries claim they're eradicating coca plantations, and they have made some progress. But the flow of cocaine into the U.S. and Europe has actually increased; they simply move or replant the crops — or cross the border and step up production in more liberal countries. Colombia and Nueva Sangria claim to be part of the eradication program but are secretly protecting coca production. Then there's the other side of the coin: the cocaleros — coca farmers — are in revolt. They claim that the U.S. has no right to dictate what they grow, and there have been numerous and violent clashes between the police and the farmers. One policeman's body was found in a shallow grave, his face eaten away by acid."

I shuddered. Kathy helped herself to more wine and refilled Trevor's glass.

"In many respects you can't blame them," Trevor continued. "Of the seventeen or so varieties of coca, only two are really good for cocaine production, and they deplete the soil, although the plant grows fairly well just about anywhere. The farmers' argument is that, if they stop growing coca, they go back to subsistence farming,

living on the edge of starvation. They have understand-
ably gotten comfortable with their gold Rolex watches
and sending their children to expensive universities.
And now they have a new outlet: some of the radical Is-
lamist groups are smuggling cocaine across the Sahara
to Europe. So until someone comes up with a crop that
brings in as much cash as coca, production of it will continue. In addition, the coca leaf in its natural state — before it's reduced to cocaine — is actually very beneficial.
Most of the natives chew it daily."

"It sounds like a nation of leaf-chewing drug ad-
dicts," the accountant said.

Trevor shook his head. "The natural leaf isn't addictive. It's a mild euphoric, yes, but it's also very beneficial
nutritionally and has been proven to increase energy
levels much more safely than caffeine. They use it to
treat altitude sickness and stomach upsets and it's still
used in religious rituals. But when coca is processed into
cocaine it loses all its positive properties and becomes
deadly. Unfortunately, the use of cocaine in that area is
on the rise, as it is in the rest of the world."

"It sounds as if you've been down there," I said.

He nodded. "About two years ago, and I have no intention of going back. Even then, I could feel the tension
— like the pressure before a huge storm. The place is a
time bomb, and eventually something'll trigger it."

"Communists?" the accountant asked.

"It's almost inevitable that fascists of some sort
would try to take over. There've been rumors and scattered violence for years, but nobody cared much about
an obscure banana republic somewhere in the middle of
South America — until oil was discovered about a year
ago, to everyone's astonishment. Just before the second
world war, lots of money was spent testing for oil, but
they didn't find any. However, with new technology, they
have determined it *is* there, and now everybody wants a
piece of the action — and, with the 'official' coca eradica-

tion, the poor people are having their land stolen from them. They have every reason to revolt. It's a damned shame they won't be able to sustain it." He sighed. "On the other hand, if they did succeed, the next government would be just as repressive as the last. Different faces, same policies."

"And I understand the place is not recommended for tourists," Vance commented. "Especially us *gringos*."

Trevor nodded. "It's really kind of sad, because there are some beautiful and very spiritual places down there. But express kidnapping has become a real problem."

"*Express* kidnapping?" Mrs. Lornigan asked.

Trevor smiled grimly. "Technology comes even to the back woods. They wait until a tourist gets into a taxi or some other isolated spot. Then they hold them prisoner for a few hours for their credit cards and cash and cell phones. They force the victims to go to an ATM and get as much cash as they can, and they go on a spending spree with the credit cards. Sometimes the victims are killed, sometimes not. And it's an escalating problem. There were 400 express kidnappings in Bolivia last year; I don't even want to think what they must be in Nueva Sangria. The poverty level there is unbelievable."

Lornigan nodded. "What they need is a good education system."

"That would help," Trevor acknowledged, "but children don't have time for school. They're out in the fields, working long hard days in the sun, as soon as they can walk. Only the very rich receive any education at all. It's not exaggeration to say the illiteracy rate is 95%. Life expectancy is something like 40 years; besides the work in the fields, the fumes from processing coca into cocaine paste are deadly. By the time they're 30, they're old, bent, and worn out."

The group was silent for a moment, contemplating the plight of a people who were virtually slaves.

"And yet the highly-educated upper class in most of

those Latino countries are very much like us," I commented.

Trevor glanced at me with new interest. "Are you Latin American?"

"My mother is Peruvian. She embraced the North American culture completely when she came here — although she insisted on speaking Spanish at home because she didn't want me to completely lose touch with my roots." I smiled ruefully. "As a result, I speak Spanish with a heavy Peruvian accent."

"You use it in your business, don't you?" Sylvia asked.

I nodded. "It's one reason I wound up carrying the line I do; I can converse with the vendors who don't speak English."

Kathy, who had, for most of the dinner, focused her attention on the wine, spoke up muzzily. "*Evr'body* oughta speak 'nglish. Makes it much easier t' comm. . . comm. . . What's 'at word, Tr'vr honey?"

"Communicate?"

"Yeah, *'at's* the one!" She punched him on the shoulder and giggled. Trevor and Sylvia exchanged glances and Sylvia rolled her eyes. There was an uncomfortable silence.

"Well," Sylvia said brightly, "I suggest we adjourn to the living room." But the pastor, having seen the exchange between Sylvia and Trevor, made a show of looking at his watch and apologized, "I'm afraid we must run. I have an important conference early tomorrow." His comment reminded the accountant that he, too, must be going, and I made similar noises.

Trevor ushered the other guests to the door while I went in search of my handbag, but Sylvia pulled me into the kitchen. "Can you stay for a while after the others leave?"

"Sure. . ."

She patted my arm and hurried to say her goodbyes. But Kathy was not about to leave. "L'es have 'nother drink," she suggested. " 'S early yet — got all night, don' we, honey? Les' have s'me champaaaagne!"

"I'd love to, Kitten, but I have a deadline to meet. I'm going to have to work most of the night," Trevor replied.

Kathy hiccoughed and giggled. "I'll help. You know me: 'm a *great* help in th' *dark*room." She giggled again, rolling her hips suggestively.

It was apparent that Sylvia and Trevor had some sort of pre-arranged plan, because Sylvia said, "Your taxi is already downstairs, Kathy. Let me help you with your wrap."

"But I wanna shtay wi' Trev'r."

"I'll walk you down to the cab and tuck you in all nice and safe," Trevor murmured as he guided her, still pro-testing, toward the door. I couldn't help but admire his aplomb in the face of her determination to "shtay'n'elp." Several minutes later he was back, disgustedly wiping lipstick off his face.

Sylvia chuckled. "My, my, how our little Kitten does blossom when she's been drinking. It's true love, Trevor — I can tell." He aimed a swat at her, which she evaded with practiced ease and a saucy grin.

"She needs to be in an institution," Trevor muttered. "I wish Bob would realize that."

Sylvia turned to me. "Kathy's family and ours have been friends forever — but she never was very stable. Since her marriage she's been hitting the bottle pretty hard, but her husband refuses to face the fact that she's an alcoholic."

"Status," Trevor said. "He can't afford the social stig-ma of having an alcoholic wife in a drying-out clinic."

"I would think that would be preferable to having her make a drunken fool of herself in public," Vance commented.

Trevor nodded agreement. "But Bob won't listen. He insists she just drinks a little too much sometimes. We've given up."

"I don't suppose it's any of my business," I interjected, "but where was her husband tonight?"

Trevor snorted. "Well, according to the official story,
he's in New York on business. I rather suspect he's with
one of his many whores."

"Oh, how sad," I replied. "No wonder she drinks.
And she's obviously extremely fond of you, Trevor. It
must be very difficult for her."

Trevor gave me a strange, hard look, but said nothing.

Sylvia laughed. "I can remember Kathy telling me,
when we were about ten, that she was going to marry
Trevor. He's been running ever since."

It was soon apparent that we had come to the real
reason for the evening, for the four of us settled into
comfortable chairs with coffee and cognac. Sylvia kicked
off her shoes, and, after a moment's hesitation, I followed suit. Before long the men had loosened their ties
and kicked shoes off, also. Sylvia put some classical guitar on the CD player, and talk was casual and aimless.

Vance discussed the construction industry, which
was doing well in spite of the weak economy. "The bean-
counters don't understand it, but the simple fact is that
people need places to live and there isn't enough hous-
ing in this city."

Trevor grinned. "Build huge dormitories. It'd be
cheaper."

"Always the pragmatist," Vance laughed.

Trevor's next words caught me by surprise. "So,
Daphne. Tell us about yourself. Aside from the fact that
you import household furnishings and your mother is
from Peru, we know nothing about you."

"I'm a wanderer and stranger," I intoned. "I come
from forever, roaming the earth."

Trevor's look of astonishment surprised me. "Do you
know the rest?" he asked sharply.

It was my turn to be astonished. "The rest of what?
I just said it to be funny. I didn't know it was part of

anything."

Staring at the floor, Trevor quoted softly,

Here I am an outcast, seeking after life,
Haunted and delighted, hiding from the sun.
Far beyond the deeds of evil men and lies,
Panting, thirsting, dying for one touch of love.
Wanderer and stranger,
I come from forever, roaming the earth,
Caught in a dream of what is beyond.

He shook his head. "It doesn't sound right in English — the original is in Spanish — but it's a beautifully lyrical and sad story of a being — entity, spirit — whatever you call it — trying to experience life on earth, but never finding love, the one thing it needs to survive. It was written around 1300 A.D. but the Church suppressed it."

Suddenly I was having trouble breathing and the hair on the back of my neck rose — because I *knew* the next verse, and before I could stop myself I was reciting in Spanish:

I will walk in shadow, I will hide from light;
Find me in the depths of ancient scrolls
For I have been here where I stand
A hundred times before,
And no man has seen my face
Or known the paths I trod.

Trevor was staring at me now, as he'd stared at me at the gala. "I thought you said you didn't know it."

I was beginning to panic. "I swear I've never heard it before in my life. It just . . . came to me, and I said the words I heard."

Nobody said anything, but I seemed to be the only one upset. Sylvia and Vance were watching with interest; Trevor had a strange smile on his face.

Finally Sylvia spoke. "Well, you were right, brother dear. She's one of us."

"One of who?" I asked. "Could I have a glass of water, please?"

Vance got up to get it while Sylvia explained. "Trevor and I have been aware for years that we've been together before, in many lifetimes. And he told me at the gala that he was quite certain that you were his wife during the Civil War. He was wounded and came home to die and Sherman —"

"Please don't say it, Sylvia," I interrupted. I was trembling, and for some reason I had to say it myself. I took a deep breath and said, "I shot Trevor, and then myself, with a shotgun. So Sherman couldn't capture us. The slaves fled to a root cellar in the woods."

I was very near tears, but Trevor and Sylvia were both grinning delightedly. I felt old and used and dirty — and suddenly I was angry again. "And I was a normal, well-balanced woman until you did whatever . . . whatever you did to me at the gala," I stormed at Trevor. "I haven't been the same since that night. I've been having nightmares, and sometimes I think I'm on the brink of madness. What right do you have to . . . to get inside women's heads like that and screw with their minds? I should have run the first time I saw you!" I was nearly shouting now, tears running down my face.

Instantly Trevor was kneeling beside me, his arms tight around me, whispering soothing words, smoothing my hair — the way I'd dreamed he would — but angry, confused and embarrassed, I pushed him away and buried my face in my hands. Finally I calmed down and, dabbing at my eyes with a tissue, I muttered, "I am truly sorry. I didn't mean to blow up like that. It's just that, since you spoke to me that night, Trevor, my whole life has been in turmoil. I've been having bad dreams which I finally learned are past-life regressions and . . . and some other scary things have happened."

"You want to tell us about it?" It was Vance, sitting next to Sylvia, calmly holding her hand.

There wasn't much point in being coy; these people obviously knew more about me than I did. I told them about the aftermath of the gala, carefully editing the scenes with Ron to "a bitter argument whose brutal overtones scared me", grateful they didn't press me for details. I told them about the dreams I'd been having, and about LuAnne's explanation. They all listened quietly, Trevor perched on the arm of my chair, his arm around my shoulders. The grown woman in me wanted to shrug him off and move out of reach; the frightened little girl in me was grateful for his reassurance.

"Wow," he said when I finally ran down. "No wonder you're angry. Jesus, to get hit with it all at once like that . . ! Believe me, if I'd known, I would have found a gentler way of approaching you. But I was so certain that we knew each other, and I just . . . I'm sorry."

I shook my head. "How were you to know?"

Sylvia spoke: "When it first started happening to Trevor and me we thought, like you, it was just dreams, but we were struck by the fact that we both had had the same dream. We started doing some reading, and that's when we realized we were reliving past lives." She smiled encouragingly. "You'll get used to it, honest."

"It does help to know I'm not alone," I admitted.

Vance laughed. "Oh, you're not alone, Daphne. The entire world is in it with you. But most of them don't know it."

8

"... And so after Sylvia and Vance went to bed Trevor and I talked until about 4:30 this morning, and then he insisted on following me home to be sure I got in safely," I told LuAnne the next afternoon on the phone.

"And?"

"And what? He kissed me on the cheek, held me tight for a moment, then unlocked my door, shooed me inside and insisted I lock it before he walked back to his car and drove away. End, as you say, of story. Sorry — no heaving bosoms, no throbbing members."

She chuckled. "No dreams?"

"None. If I did dream, I was too wiped out to remember."

"What'd you talk about?"

"Mostly about past lives and other metaphysical stuff. He and Sylvia are pretty heavily into it. If he's right, we — as spirits, or, as he calls them, entities — form kind of a spiritual family and keep reincarnating together, always in different relationships but always together, with different lessons to learn."

"Yeah, there's some evidence for that, which would explain why you both felt you knew each other the first time you met. You apparently *did*."

"He said we were brothers in nineteenth-century Russia. I was killed in a train wreck when I was ten and he was twelve. He was with his — our — parents when they identified my body. Many of the injured froze to death before they could be rescued, and he was horrified at the sight of frozen bodies all over the place. He had a lot of guilt to work through in that lifetime because he was supposed to have gone with me and refused. I was traveling alone, to visit our grandmother."

"You gonna see him again?"

"Probably. I think he's worried about me after my outburst last night, and wants to be more careful. But we agreed we need to get together and explore this."

"I smell something hot!" LuAnne crowed.

I grinned. "Maybe. We'll see. I'll admit that, after my initial jumpiness, his arms felt very good around me — like they belonged there."

I could hear her chuckle as we rang off.

❧　❦

Later that day my phone rang. Assuming it was Trevor, I couldn't keep the breathless expectation out of my voice.

"Daphne — you sound much better!" It was Ron.

I kept my voice carefully neutral. "I am. Thanks."

"Look, I know what you said last time, but I really think we need to discuss this." Before I could reply, he hurried on, "I'm worried about you, and I feel it was my fault. I'll be back in town Wednesday to finalize things there, and I'd like to take you to dinner. No pressure — no commitments. I simply want to reassure myself that you're okay."

"I can't. I have something on that evening."

"I'll be in town until Friday. Can we do it Thursday, then?"

I sighed in exasperation. "You're making this very difficult for me."

"I just need to see you again. Is that so wrong?"

The plaintive note in his voice brought my rage to the surface, and I suppose I was crueler than I should have been. "Yes, it is wrong. I'm fine now, and I'd like to stay that way. Let's not pick at old wounds — just let them heal."

"Have I done something wrong, Daphne?"

"It's not you. I've changed a lot lately and I no longer think we're meant for each other. I sincerely hope you find a wonderful woman who will make you happy. But I'm not that woman."

"Daphne, give me a chance!" I could hear the tears in his voice.

"Let it go, Ron. Please let it go."

"But. . ."

I put the phone down.

Less than thirty seconds later, it rang again. Swearing under my breath, I picked it up. *"Now what!?"*

"Daphne? It's Trevor."

"Oh, Trevor, I'm sorry. I just hung up from an unpleasant conversation with someone else and I thought they were calling back."

"Jesus! Remind me not to get you mad at me — again."

I laughed. "It's good to hear your voice. Did you sleep well?"

"Honestly? No. I spent the night thinking about you."

"Yeah, right. I'll bet you say that to all your women."

"Not all of them — just the special ones."

"Well, at least I've moved from the 'demented' category to the 'special' category — or do they mean the same thing in your lexicon?"

"I'd rather not answer that," he chuckled. "Can you

spare some time from your busy schedule to have dinner with me tonight? I realize it's short notice, but my ego is so big I'm sure you'll be delighted to cancel any plans you might have and throw yourself into my eager arms."

"God, it's a good thing you don't write that stuff for publication. You'd starve to death."

"I only talk that way to my special women."

"All of them? And does that mean I have to listen to that junk all evening?"

"Not if you don't have dinner with me." Without giving me a chance to reply, he added, "I'll pick you up about 6:00."

I glanced at my watch. "Isn't that kind of early?"

"Frankly, my beloved sister had all she could do to keep me from pounding on your door at 9:00 this morning. I can't stand the strain much longer."

I laughed. "Trevor Elliot, you are disgusting! What shall I wear? Satin and lace? Jeans?"

"How about a black teddy?"

"I don't even own one." Which wasn't true, but that was none of his business.

He let out a gusty melodramatic sigh. "I guess jeans will have to do, then. I wasn't planning anything fancy; I don't even know where we'll go. I just need to see you."

This time I could hear the honesty in his voice, and I reflected how wonderful that sounded coming from Trevor, while the same phrase, coming from Ron, made me want to kill.

In the end, we brought Chinese carry-out back to my place, both of us too tired after last night to dress for a nice restaurant, neither of us willing to put up with the noise of a less formal place. Sprawled on the living room floor with our "picnic" between us, we sipped wine and talked.

"Sylvia and I were orphaned when we were six," he told me.

I nodded. "She told me. It must have been awful for

you, you were so young!"

"We were really very lucky. Mother's parents were good people and they were always there for us, especially the first few years after the plane crash, when we were still trying to deal with the fact that Mom and Dad weren't coming home. Sylvia would wake up crying and crawl into bed with me, but then she'd get me crying. I never figured out how grandmother knew, but she always appeared about that time, no matter how quiet we tried to be. She'd hold us or pull us into bed with her until we settled down.

"I remember the day Sylvia, trying to be very grown-up and logical, explained to grandmother that it might be easier if we called them Mom and Dad. Mom — grandmother — burst into tears and Sylvia thought she'd said something wrong. It took us quite some time to sort things out. Grandmother's tears were tears of joy, and they've been Mom and Dad ever since."

"Are they still alive?"

"Mom is. Dad passed away about ten years ago, but Mom is still quite active, although she walks with a cane. I inherited my writing from her. She still keeps a daily journal — has since she learned how to write. She was my first editor, and, Jesus, was she a curmudgeon! She'd make me go over every word until I had it perfect."

"I'll bet you resented that."

He smiled. "Not really. I understood from the beginning that she was trying to hone a talent I had anyhow, and I've always been grateful, even when I thought she was being unreasonable. I had to completely rewrite one essay four times before she was satisfied — but her training stood me in good stead later. I've had several editors comment that my work needs very little editing, and when they do suggest changes, I don't get defensive and angry like so many writers do. I realize they're trying to make my work as readable — and saleable— as possible, so I make as many changes as I'm comfortable with, and they're usually happy with the finished product."

"The one piece I read was impressive."

"I didn't know you'd read any of my stuff."

"I happened to read an article by you in a news magazine in the dentist's waiting room. It triggered one of those past-life dreams, by the way. I hate to admit I don't even remember what country it was about — but I remember the picture of the two tots with their arms around each other. God, that's a haunting picture!"

"They haunt me still. They were so young and couldn't understand why their world was in such chaos. They reminded me a little of Sylvia and myself. We survived; they didn't. Why? Who makes the decision that a couple of WASP kids in America survive the loss of their parents and never miss a meal, while kids like that — who are just as deserving of a good life — starve to death or get caught in a gun battle? Why don't they get the same chance we did?"

I didn't know what to say. He fidgeted with the wine bottle cork as he fought with his emotions, and I didn't have the courage to touch and reassure him as I wanted to — as he had done for me the night before. Finally he glanced up with an apologetic smile. "Sorry. I get carried away."

"I'm not surprised. You've seen an awful lot in your life — and quite frankly, I would worry about you if you *didn't* have some emotional baggage as a result. At least you're a normal human being."

"Am I? And what, O Divine Dispenser of Wisdom and Chinese Carry-Out, is a normal human being?"

I laughed. "Somebody who agrees with all my views on life."

"That is one scary criterion," he replied, grinning at me with open admiration.

I dropped my eyes. "Mamá used to say I'd go far in life because I was so sure of my sight. If she could see the way I've been acting since I met you, she wouldn't be so confident."

"You'll get over it. It just hit you all at once, and you're still assimilating it." He took my hand and studied it. "I need to get Sylvia to look at your palm. I'm not too good at that kind of thing, but I can see some real determination in you."

I smiled. "I'm afraid you're wrong. In spite of being so sure of my sight, as Mamá put it, I'm not particularly aggressive." — *except for that disaster with Ron* — "I usually take the passive approach."

"That doesn't mean you're not determined. You go at it obliquely, rather than approaching things head-on."

"Maybe you're right. I never thought about it."

"You couldn't have made a success of your business if you hadn't been determined," Trevor pointed out.

"Actually, the reason I went into business for myself was cowardice. I worked for an architectural firm for a few years after college. They spent more time bickering and back-stabbing than designing buildings. I couldn't imagine spending the rest of my life playing politics."

Trevor nodded. "I never even tried working for someone else. I've been writing and publishing since I was a kid, thanks to Mom, and it made sense to add photography to my résumé and go freelance. I've never regretted it."

"Obviously you've done well. You were surrounded by admirers all evening at the gala."

He grinned. "All of them thinking I was somebody powerful who could do them a favor. The truth is a freelancer is only as powerful as the current assignment. If I blow an assignment, I don't have an understanding boss to give me another chance and keep paying the bills whether I produce or not. Word gets around fast in that industry. Write a lousy article or make a political mistake, and suddenly you're writing jingles for the local college radio station. If you're lucky."

"It must get kind of scary sometimes."

"I don't let myself think about it much. I take an assignment, hop a plane, and snap pictures." He played with my fingers, examining my rings, matching his palm to mine, chuckling when he realized my hands and feet — inherited from my Scandinavian father — were nearly as big as his. I hoped he couldn't feel the tremor in my arm when he touched me.

"According to Sylvia, you put your heart and soul into your work," I commented.

"She's been very patient with me."

"The affection between you two fascinates me. I have a brother and two sisters, but we're nowhere near as close as you and Sylvia. I haven't seen or heard from my brother for years."

"We're so much a part of each other I don't think the other would survive if one of us died." He grinned. "On the other hand, we both know we'll probably spend the next lifetime together in some relationship or other, so it's not likely we'll lose each other for all eternity."

I swallowed envy. This was love on a level I could only guess at. And would there be, I wondered, a place in Trevor's heart for me?

It was almost as if he read my thoughts, for he kissed my palm solemnly and said, "And I suspect you'll be there, too. You have been, in so many of my lives. I'm glad I found you in this one."

I couldn't think of anything to say. I was afraid to break the spell, but I was also aware of that strange sense of foreboding again. His touch set every nerve in my body jangling, and I couldn't understand my fear, although I suspected it had something to do with my attacking Ron. Would Trevor also find himself in harm's way?

I pulled away, and he seemed to understand my emotions, for he released my hand and murmured, "I think it's time for me to go."

I was astonished to see it was well after midnight. He stood up and stretched like a huge predatory cat. I shivered and began gathering up cartons and dishes. He helped clean up and pulled the bag out of the trash can. "Where do you put your garbage? You don't want this smelling up your kitchen tonight."

I led him out the back door and pointed to the trash bin. The night was deliciously cool, the moon nearly full, making the small fenced yard look otherworldly — lawn chairs became headstones, the tiny lawn a moonscape. I shivered again and suddenly his arms were warm around me. "You cold?" he murmured into my hair.

"I don't know what I am, Trevor Elliot. You trigger the strangest sensations in me." But I returned his embrace, wondering at the *rightness* of the way it felt. And suddenly he was inside my head again, a gentle, amused, loving presence. I wanted to be afraid, but I couldn't muster the energy. Instead we stood in silence, soaking up the strange bliss.

Finally, gently, he pushed me away. "If I don't go now, I'll not be responsible for my actions. Throw me out, *cara mia*."

I kissed him quickly and led him around the side of the house to his car, afraid if I said a word I'd beg him to stay — and I was terrified of a replay of the scene with Ron. But how long could I keep Trevor at arm's length without losing him entirely?

He gave me a brotherly hug and kiss and I stood watching in the moonlight until his car's taillights disappeared around the corner.

9

LuAnne took one look at me Monday morning and burst into delighted laughter. "Well, it's apparent you had a good weekend!"

"You read me like a book," I grumbled good-naturedly.

"Hard not to. You look like a cat that's been smothered in cream."

I smiled sheepishly. "I guess that's kind of how I feel."

"So tell me all about it."

I shrugged. "Not much to tell. We spent Saturday and Sunday evenings together, just talking. He has some stories to tell! But, you know, simply being with him is relaxing. With Ron, I always felt I had to prove myself, live up to some vague and high expectations — although he never hinted at anything of the sort; it was just a kind of tension that he evoked in me. I suspect part of it was that I was quite sure his family would be less than delighted with his interest in a *Latina* half-breed. On the other hand, Trevor is like an old comfortable pair of shoes or a warm sweater. Ron was by Pierre Cardin; Trevor is one of those solid, wearable brands you buy at Sears."

"So you want to dance among the stars, but you want to do it in comfortable shoes."

"Exactly. He does make me dance in the stars, but we still have our feet firmly planted on the ground. So far."

Just then the phone rang. "It's a Mr. Trevor Elliot for you. Is he a new business associate?" LuAnne asked with deadpan innocence. She suppressed laughter when I nearly broke her wrist grabbing the phone, then, still chuckling, made a show of going into the next room and closing the door behind her.

"Good morning, Mr. Elliot. How are you?"

"Panting, thirsting, dying for one touch of love from one very special lady. Did you sleep well?"

"I did. And you?"

I heard him chuckle. "I guess I'm getting paid back for your sleepless nights."

"Good — you deserve it," I laughed. "What kept you awake?"

"You mean you don't know? You, of course."

"C'mon — we hardly know each other."

"We've known each other for millennia. The only part of you that I don't know is the part that's new to this lifetime."

"Are you serious?"

"Sure. Since I could see I wasn't going to get you out of my mind anyhow, I spent most of the night doing research on other lives we've spent together."

"I'm afraid to ask how you do that." I stared out the window, watching two birds in a spring mating ritual.

"It's not hard. I'll teach you, if you'd like. You go into a meditative trance and . . . well, sort of go looking." I heard what sounded like a snicker from his end. "Jesus, you should've seen what we did in Cincinnati!"

"I've never been to Cincinnati."

"Oh, yes you have. It was about fifty years after the Civil War. You were married to a prosperous merchant — hardware, I think. You lived in a big mansion on the river outside the city. He used to travel a lot, and you got lonely."

"Were you my husband?"

"Oh, no. I was the local banker. Bankers in those days didn't travel much; they were too busy keeping an eye on their money. But I did a lot of heavy consulting with a certain lovely and lonely client." He was laughing now. "There was one afternoon on the piano bench — you still play the piano, by the way?"

"No. . ."

"Well, you were playing it with your heels that afternoon."

"Trevor!" In spite of myself I was laughing. "You're making this all up."

"No, it was as real as the time you took Antonius' head off — which was a pretty gross thing to do, by the way."

"Well, you know what they say: when in Rome. . ."

"Yeah, but taunting him afterwards. . ." he chuckled.

"How did you know about that? I don't remember telling you."

"You didn't; I was Myrah, remember?"

I didn't want to think too carefully about that. "Well, remember that if you ever decide to cross me."

"Yes, ma'am. I most surely will. Now, to the reason I'm calling. This isn't a social call, you know."

"Oh, pardon me. What can I do for you, Mr. Elliot?"

"My secretary left town with the banker or I would have had her call to set up a luncheon date today. It's most urgent that I see you, Ms. Morris."

"I see. Would you like to speak with my secretary? We really must stick to proprieties."

To my surprise, he said yes and, grinning, I buzzed LuAnne. "Mr. Elliot would like to speak to my secretary to set up a luncheon engagement," I told her gaily. "His secretary is out of town or he would have had her call."

LuAnne picked up the phone without missing a beat. Curiosity kept me on the line. "Mr. Elliot, this is LuAnne Blackwell, private secretary to Ms. Morris. How may I help you?"

"Ms. Morris is in need of some special counseling on past lives, which, I understand, you have some knowledge of. In view of the urgency of this situation, please cancel any luncheon engagements she may have and schedule an appointment at 1:00 with me every day for the foreseeable future."

"Wait I minute," I broke in. "I have a business to run. Wednesday afternoon I have to meet with one of my clients, and Thursday I'm having lunch with a potential supplier."

Trevor sighed one of his gusty theatrical sighs. "Really, Ms. Morris, you apparently don't understand the urgency of this situation. Nevertheless, Ms. Blackwell, if you will be so *kind* as to schedule luncheon appointments with me for the days she can *possibly* spare the time, I'd be *most* grateful."

"Of course, sir. Will there be anything else?"

"No — you've been a good sport. Thanks."

"Have a good day, Mr. Elliot. You've already made mine." And LuAnne, laughing, hung up.

And so went the next few weeks. I reflected with wry amusement that, even before that disastrous evening with Ron, if he had insisted on seeing me as much as Trevor did, I would have told him off. Instead, I looked forward to every moment Trevor and I were together. I had been a neat-freak all my life, but suddenly laundry and dishes went undone and my correspondence piled up — and every time Trevor called, I happily dropped everything, wondering at my sudden adolescence.

One evening I followed him around at a meet-and-greet for one of the newspaper bigwigs. I shook hands with the guest of honor and promptly forgot his name. Mostly I stood around while Trevor, in what Sylvia called his Party Boy Mode, chatted with friends and strangers alike. I was never sure which was which; he appeared to know everybody.

But I was enjoying myself, watching him work the crowd like a politician. He shook hands with almost everyone, always with a word or joke or a funny aside. My arm got tired from shaking hands, because he insisted on introducing me to everyone he spoke to. I was beginning to feel like a celebrity myself — and then I saw Ron. I was looking for a bolt hole when he spotted me. Any hopes I had that he might snub me out of spite were dashed when he came straight for me, a welcoming, questioning smile on his face. Trevor had his back to me at the moment, deep in conversation with two of the newspaper's senior editors, so I must have looked as if I was alone.

"Daphne, I didn't expect to see you here."

"Uh, hello, Ron. I didn't expect to see you, either. I thought you were back in Miami. How are you?"

"I'm in town a few days to finalize some things. But more to the point, how are *you*? Are you okay?" He studied me as if I were a patient recently released from Intensive Care — or the psycho ward. "I've been very worried about you."

"I'm fine, thanks." And I had not a clue what to say after that.

"Is Country Cuzzin doing all right?" Ron seemed genuinely concerned.

I tried to brush it off. "There were some rough times, but we seem to be pulling out of it fairly well. I'm about to sign a contract with the firm doing the interiors for LakePointe. That helps."

About that time Trevor turned and said, "Daphne, I'd like you to meet two of my partners in crime. . ." The look on my face stopped him cold, and then he became aware of Ron. I had to give Trevor credit; he hardly missed a beat, but smiled and extended his hand. "I believe we met at the Harmon Gala. Nice to see you again."

Ron ignored Trevor's hand. Instead, he looked at me with something close to contempt. "I see." He started to speak to Trevor, thought better of it, and without another word turned on his heel and stalked off.

"Rather poor timing, eh?" Trevor murmured. "I hope I didn't ruin anything."

I couldn't the grin off my face. "Actually, you probably did, but it's something I've been trying to ruin for weeks now. So, thank you." I looked up at him. "There's no competition, Trevor. None."

His smile warmed me clear down to my toes. "I never doubted it, *cara mia*. If I'm reading you right, I think this deserves champagne." He put his arm around me, introduced me briefly to the two editors, and led me to the bar. I didn't see Ron again that evening.

Or ever.

But I saw Trevor every chance I got. Frequently we had dinner with Sylvia and Vance. Although not necessarily sharing the Elliots' fascination with past lives, Vance was quite at ease with the subject, and I suspected his interest went deeper than he admitted. Certainly his love for Sylvia was strong, and returned in full measure. It was fun to watch them together, and, as Sylvia had said, I could detect no jealousy between Vance and Trevor, only affection and mutual respect. If I hadn't known better, I might have thought they were brothers.

One evening Sylvia remarked to me that she was glad I didn't appear to be jealous of the bond between her and Trevor.

"I'm really boiling inside. I just hide it well," I joked.

"Bull," Vance retorted. "I've been watching you watch the twins. You think it's wonderful — as I do."

"It's a relationship I can only guess at, but, yes, it is fun, although I admit I'm also a bit envious. It would never happen with any of my siblings."

"I've been watching for signs of jealousy," Trevor admitted. "It always seems to come up when either Sylvia or I start a new relationship. But either it's not there, or you're hiding it well."

"I told you, I'm really boiling inside." But I didn't try to hide my grin. "Actually, I can't see any reason for jealousy. Sylvia obviously fills some need in you — and you in her — that Vance and I can't fill. I'm fine with that, and from what I've seen, so is Vance."

Vance nodded. "Actually, I think Sylvia's bond with Trevor enhances my relationship with her, although I'm not sure I can explain how or why."

"There's no way one human being can be the perfect mate, and, to be honest, I wouldn't want to be," I replied. "I'm a human with my own needs and desires; there will always be gaps in any relationship — needs that must be met elsewhere. If one person starts believing they must be all things to another person, they've left the arena of love and gotten into something sick. I'm delighted that you have her, Trevor, and still have room in your life for me and your work, which, according to Sylvia, consumes you —"

"That's the understatement of the century," she muttered.

" — and *that* takes a very special kind of person," I finished.

Trevor looked at me with huge mock-sorrowful eyes. "You mean you're not going to give up your business and stay barefoot and pregnant for me?"

"Don't even think about it."

"Nice try, brother," Sylvia laughed. "I think you've got the wrong woman."

"Actually, she's already barefoot. . ." Vance interjected. As usual, all four of us had our shoes off and were sprawled on the floor or the couch. There was an embarrassed silence. "Hey, I was only joking!"

The truth was that I didn't know how Trevor felt

about the physical side of our relationship. Our discussions were far-ranging, but this was one subject we avoided. There was no doubt in my mind — or in his, I was sure — that our affection for each other grew daily. But when the affection threatened to turn to passion, he always backed off. Part of me was relieved, for I was not interested in casual sex — and I had not yet recovered from the horror of that night with Ron, still harboring a secret fear that I might do the same to Trevor. Certainly he aroused me, and there were many times when we were on the verge of tumbling into bed, but there was an old-fashioned gallantry in him, and perhaps he was reluctant to trespass. Or maybe he simply didn't find me physically attractive, in which case our relationship would eventually dissolve, an eventuality I didn't want to dwell on. Neither of us was in a hurry to find out.

                   ❧ ❦

I'd spent most of the afternoon pretending to do paperwork, but Trevor West Elliot's face superimposed itself on invoices, his voice whispered in my ear, his laughter echoed in the whir of the printer. Several times I distinctly felt his presence, so much so that once I actually glanced over my shoulder, expecting to see him standing there. I was working on the third — or was it the fourth? — revision of an invoice when LuAnne declared loudly, "Oxygen deprivation."

I jumped. I hadn't heard her come in. "What?"

"I've been talking to you for several minutes and you haven't heard a word I said. You're so far up in the stratosphere you're suffering from oxygen deprivation."

I scratched one bare foot with the other and smiled sheepishly. "Guilty as charged. I'm having trouble concentrating."

She glanced at the invoice I was holding. "No kidding. Did you know Townsend Enterprises doesn't ever buy soap dishes from us? They buy reception room furnishings. And they haven't bought anything at all for months."

I sighed and threw the invoice in the trash. "I might as well give up. I don't think I've accomplished a thing all afternoon."

"Good. I've been looking for an excuse to carry you away from this menial drudgery." It was Trevor — for real this time — grinning at us from the doorway, dressed in khakis and hiking boots, a bush hat cocked jauntily over one eye. My heart did a funny flip. "I hope I'm not interrupting anything." He glanced at LuAnne and said, "And this must be the redoubtable Ms. Blackwell. Pleased to make your acquaintance at last." Sweeping off his hat, he bowed low, Shakespearean style.

LuAnne smiled and curtsied with as much stagey coquettishness as she could manage in shorts and sleeveless blouse. "Likewise. But would you do me a favor and get her out of here? She's worse than useless."

"Hey, I'm the senior partner, remember?" I squawked.

"Yes, ma'am, absolutely ma'am. I have great admiration for you as my boss, but loyalty forces me to say, with all due respect, ma'am, that you're worse than useless. Now will you please go away?" She handed me my shoes and pointed to the door.

I laughed. "Trevor, since I don't get no respect here, perhaps you'd be kind enough to get me out of here, per my partner's request."

"At your service." And he gallantly offered me his arm, escorting me to his car.

"Where are we going?"

"Have you had lunch?"

"I vaguely remember LuAnne force-feeding me something a while ago. Why?"

"I thought a quiet walk in the woods might be good for both of us. But you'll need to put your shoes on."

"It's been years since I walked in trees. It sounds wonderful." *How does he always seem to know what I need?*

A national park was a short drive away, and we rode in companionable silence. I enjoyed just being with him, aware of his masculine presence, letting the warm afternoon breeze soak the tension out of me.

At the park he shouldered a backpack and took my hand. "There's a beautiful stream about half a mile off the path. Is that too far for you to walk?"

"If I say yes, will you carry me?"

"Nope. But I'll let you sit in the car by yourself until I get back."

He headed into the trees and I had to trot to keep up with his long-legged strides. Finally I objected, "Hey, you said a walk, not a forced march."

"Sorry. I forgot about your short legs."

The stream, dancing joyfully among rocks, was full and noisy. Trevor led me across stepping stones to a huge flat boulder in the middle where we sat and let the peace soak through us. Sunlight peeked through overhanging trees and sparkled on the water roaring around us. We had to shout to hear each other, but we were both content with not speaking. I thought of the old poem, "If once you have slept on an island, you'll never be quite the same." It wasn't quite an island, and I doubted we'd be sleeping here, but I certainly hadn't been the same since I met this man.

Trevor unpacked his camera and I watched in fascination as the photographer in him came alive and measured light and angles and distances. He reminded me of a symphony conductor. Suddenly he looked at me. "Don't move and don't smile." Then he raised his camera and snapped several pictures as he maneuvered to get different angles.

"Why'd you tell me not to smile?"

"You look sort of waif-like, with your hair all mussed,

sitting on a rock in the middle of a stream with that puzzled expression on your face. A smile would've ruined the effect."

Then he packed up his camera and pulled me to my feet. "Ready to walk?"

"If I say no, I suppose you'll leave me here, too."

He grinned and helped me negotiate the stepping stones to the farther shore. Then we were off down a shady path. In moments the sound of the stream had faded and the hush was broken only by our footsteps and an occasional fly zooming by. Walking softly under a dim canopy of sun-flecked leaves, we spoke in hushed tones, as if in a cathedral. Somewhere a bird trilled, then abruptly fell quiet, embarrassed by its own enthusiasm.

We came upon a small glade bathed in golden sunlight. It seemed to shimmer, as if it had just been beamed down from heaven. I stopped short, staring, afraid to breathe. I half expected to see elves dancing under the trees. Trevor glanced at me and grinned. "I never would have taken you to be a wood nymph. You look as if you're enjoying yourself."

"I am. I used to love to walk in the woods, but in this day and age it's not a good idea for a woman to do it alone. There's a certain peace among trees that doesn't happen anywhere else, though. And this little glade is absolutely enchanting."

"I hesitated to share it with you. It's very special to me, and I think it would have been ruined for me if you hadn't liked it. You have to experience it when the sun is just right."

"It's lovely, Trevor," I whispered, afraid to break the magic spell. "Thank you for trusting me enough to share it."

Somewhere in the distance an alto saxophone wept. Without thinking, I raised my head to listen.

Trevor glanced at me. "What?"

"Do you hear a saxophone?"

"No. . ." He had turned to face me and was watching me with obvious fascination. "Do you?"

"Uh-huh. In the distance. . ." Then I remembered. "I heard an alto sax the first time I met you, and for the first few days after we met, I kept hearing it almost constantly. All I could think of was honey or bourbon and black velvet. It drove me a little crazy."

Trevor put his arms around me, pulling me close, and for a slice of eternity we stood, basking in the peace and the magic and each other. "That was from a past life," he finally said quietly. "We were together in Paris in the early twentieth century. The saxophone was still a fairly new instrument. I earned a meager living playing it in bars and nightclubs. That's where we met. You used to sit in the back and drink bourbon straight, and you always wore black velvet. I don't know where the honey came from. New to me."

"That's what your voice sounded like the first time I heard it. Warm and low, liquid velvet and honey."

Trevor grinned at me. "And I thought I was the only one cursed with flowery language."

The trees and sun smiled down at us. With my ear pressed against his chest, I could hear his heart beating in rhythm with my own. Trevor smelled of clean masculine sweat and soap. He bent to kiss me then, and there was a strength, a sweetness, an urgency that had never been there before. We were lost in the same wilderness of silence we had shared at the gala, a mysterious pulsation that spoke of unfathomable power. I was aware he was inside my head, but I was inside his. We were, in ways I could never explain, one. Insanely, I wanted him then and there — and I knew he felt the same urgency, for abruptly he gasped and pulled away. "I'm sorry, *cara mia,* I got carried away."

But I locked my arms around him. "Trevor Elliot, don't you ever apologize for feeling like that about me. Don't you think I feel it, too?"

He didn't say anything for a long time, his face buried in my hair. "I hoped you did; I wasn't sure. You get to a certain point and then I can sense you beginning to panic. The last thing I want to do is force myself on you."

So he *had* sensed my fear. "Something . . . happened . . . just after we first met. I'm still dealing with it and the emotional aftermath."

"Did those things have anything to do with our meeting?" he probed gently, tilting my head back and kissing my throat.

I sighed. "I think so. I'm not sure."

"Want to talk about it?"

"No. Yes. I don't know." I hesitated, trying to decide how much I dared tell him, not yet ready to share my/ Deborah's hatred of Ron/Mordecai. "Well, the night I met you, you somehow triggered a . . . a raging violence in me that was never there before. I don't know how I knew you did it, but it scared hell out of me."

He was studying me now, listening carefully. "Did the violence have to do with that guy you were with at Harmon's gala? The one you ran into at the newspaper do?"

"He was the target, but it wasn't his fault. Not really. He just . . . I dunno . . . he didn't do anything, and suddenly I was on the verge of killing him. It's all pretty confused, and putting it into words makes it sound so stupid — but he was in real danger that day, and I was driven by an anger I didn't understand. I once considered marrying him, and now I can't stand the sight or the sound of him. And I'm afraid —" I broke off.

"Afraid of what?"

"Afraid the same thing will happen if I get too close to you. God knows I love you more than I ever thought possible, but what you do to me scares the living daylights out of me. I can't explain it even to myself. And I guess I'm afraid I'll lose you if I can't get over this." My voice wavered on tears.

Trevor held me for a long time, rocking me gently, soothing me, saying nothing. Then, "Neither of us can guarantee it won't happen again," he said softly, "but I don't think it will. I think your fury was due to the fact that you knew, on some deep level, that you were with the wrong guy and you transferred your resentment to him." He chuckled, still holding me close against his chest. "And deep inside, Daphne Morris, you're still very much a warrior. Somehow our meeting triggered those warrior instincts. I wish I'd known what effect our meeting would have on you; I'd have gone more softly. But in the end we were destined to meet; you know that now."

I nodded, suddenly calm. I let out a deep, shuddering sigh and said, "Thank you."

"For what? Scaring the living daylights out of you?"

"For everything. For obeying your instincts and speaking to me that night. For explaining everything so clearly. Mostly for being the wonderful man you are."

"I wish you knew how sweet those words are coming from you."

Then he kissed me and the world went away again.

10

On the trek back to the car, Trevor spoke very little. Busy with my own inner dialogue, I left him to his, part of me marveling that we could be so comfortable with the silences. Ron would have needed to fill them up with idle prattle.

It was dark by the time we reached the car. I had no idea how long we'd been in the woods, and I was reluctant to re-enter the twenty-first century. Instead of turning on the ignition, Trevor stared at me, his eyes dark hollows in the dim light. "If you only knew," he whispered huskily, "what this day has meant to me."

I touched his face, drawing my fingers down his cheek, enjoying his shiver at my touch. "I know because it has been special for me, too. I don't know what happened. All I know is that something wonderful did. Thank you for my day."

He kissed me then, softly, gently. "I have a favor to ask."

I nodded and waited.

"I have to leave Wednesday for Los Angeles. I won't

be gone long — only a few days. Then I've an assignment to cover the Grand Prix in Monte Carlo. Will you come with me? We can take a couple of weeks, get to know each other. I want to make our first time something special, *cara* — not some grubby coupling in the back seat of a car, but a moment — a special moment out of time and space — ours alone."

From out of my childhood came the words from the book of Ruth: "Whither thou goest, my love, I shall go. Where thou lodgest, I shall lodge. Thy people shall be my people, and thy gods my gods."

His arms tightened around me. "May you never regret those words."

As Trevor started the car, police lights began flashing behind us. He chuckled and rolled down his window.

"What is it?" I asked.

"Park police. We're supposed to be out of here by dark. There's been a lot of deer poaching in here and they get very jumpy when somebody stays past curfew."

The policeman shined a bright flashlight in our faces. "The park closes at dark, sir. May I ask what you're doing here?" Before Trevor could reply, he added, "Oh, Mr. Elliot. I didn't recognize your car. Late photography session?" His light flashed on my face, blinding me.

"Sorry, Sergeant. We lost track of time and were deep in the woods when the sun started to set. Do you need to search the car?"

"No, that's okay. I don't think we'll find anything other than what we usually do. But it would be best if you'd leave immediately."

"I understand. Sorry for the inconvenience. It's hard to get out of those trees; I'd like to spend the night there."

"Jesus, don't even think about it! The lieutenant'd have my ass! Just get out of here."

Trevor grinned. "On our way. Have a good evening!"

But I noticed the patrol car followed us until we exited the park.

On the way home, he said, "There's a hotel in Monte Carlo I've visited but never stayed in. Offhand, I can't remember the name of it, but I have it somewhere in my notes. It's a beautiful old thing, full of ancient grandeur and snobbery. I'd like for us to stay there. You can relax by the pool while I cover the race, then we'll have the rest of the time to enjoy each other."

"What if I want to go to the race?"

"I wouldn't think you'd be interested."

"Why not? I've always wanted to go to a Grand Prix. Don't you need someone to tote your equipment?"

He turned to study me in the glow of the headlights. "Are you serious?"

"Of course."

"Where have you been all my life?" he asked.

"Waiting for you to show up, dummy. Took you long enough."

"Bring some evening gowns; I want to show you off. We'll do the casinos, splurge outrageously on fine wines and dinners, and spend our nights enjoying each other. I want to give you time to think about this, get used to the idea, put your fears aside."

"Do you think through all your seductions this carefully?"

"Most of them aren't worth thinking about at all," he replied.

          ॐ   ॐ

Trevor bade me good-bye Tuesday night, saying he was leaving on the early-morning flight and wouldn't call until he got to Los Angeles late that evening. Wednesday I woke up feeling as if I'd lost a part of myself, but the workaholic in me was still there, and I found a strange peace in knowing that, if the phone rang, it would be business, and no charming woodsman would material- ize to tempt me away from my responsibilities. I spent the day working on a marketing plan; I was going to have to go back to cold calling and I needed to update my pitch. LuAnne left around 5:00 to feed her six cats and hours later Trevor called, weariness ragged in his voice.

"You sound as if you walked to L.A.," I commented.

"I feel that way. We were delayed taking off by mechanical problems, which meant I missed my connecting flight. I had barely enough time to get my tickets switched and run for the next flight. I was lucky they had a seat; it was the last one for L.A. today. Now I'm sitting all alone in my hotel room, feeling edgy and irritable and very lonely. And I haven't even had dinner."

"Poor baby. That's what you get for being a globe-trotting camera jockey. Just think — if you worked in a factory, you'd be able to look forward to a quiet evening at home in front of the TV."

Trevor groaned. "With a beer balanced on my pot belly. And bored silly. Spare me. What did you do today to keep from going out of your mind without my scintillating presence?"

"It was nice and quiet for a change," I joked, careful to let him hear the laughter in my voice. "I do miss you, but I've been deeply involved in updating my sales pitch. I hope to call on several potential clients in the next couple days."

We chatted about nothing, enjoying the sound of each other's voice. Finally I said, "You need to get something to eat and get to bed. What time is your shoot tomorrow?"

"I want to be on site by 7:30, although the interview isn't until 9:00. I don't know when I'll be able to call again. With the time difference, you'll be asleep by the time I finish up for the day. I'll be back late Friday night, but it will take me a week or so to whip the article into shape and Photoshop the pictures, so you won't see much of me until late next week. I need to stay in working mode until the project is finished. Otherwise I lose momentum and the quality goes downhill fast."

"Sylvia explained that to me. She said you come home from these assignments looking and smelling as if you'd been sleeping under bridges, so I don't particularly want to see you until the transformation back to Dr. Jekyll is complete. Just call me and let me know you got back in town safely."

"I need to speak to my sister about telling all my secrets," he chuckled. "In any case, we should have the next weekend together, then a week later we leave for Monte Carlo. Are you excited?"

"I guess I don't quite believe it yet. I've always had a private superstition that if you look forward to something too much, it'll get taken away from you."

"This won't. I promise. Sleep well and I'll call when I can."

"Trevor? I . . . please remember how much I care."

"There's no way I could ever forget, *cara mia*. You haunt my dreams and light up my days. Sleep well, lady mine."

❧　❧

But it was Sylvia who called, in tears, Friday evening. "Daphne, Trevor asked me to call you; he didn't have time. Mom — our grandmother, the one who raised us — has had a stroke and isn't expected to live. I'm leaving for the airport now, and Trevor is flying directly to New Haven."

"Oh, Sylvia, I'm sorry! Is there anything at all I can do?"

"I don't think so. It's not entirely unexpected, but I still . . . we're both going to miss her."

"Does Vance know?"

"He's on his way to take me to the airport. Trevor told me to apologize and tell you he'll call when he can."

"I understand. Please let him know I'll be thinking

about both of you, and to call if there's anything I can do on this end."

I heard a sob and Sylvia replied, "Thanks, Daphne. I'll be in touch." Then she hung up.

❧   ❧

I waited anxiously as the hours passed, trying to calculate when Trevor might arrive in New Haven, but I had no idea when he'd left L.A. or what the connections would be. It was Sunday afternoon when he finally called, exhausted and near tears.

"Forgive me, Daphne. I've been at the hospital since I arrived. They let us stay with her through the night."

"How is she doing?"

There was a pause, and I knew he was fighting for control. "She died early this morning."

"Oh, Trevor, I'm so sorry. Were you and Sylvia with her?"

"Yes. She couldn't speak, but she held both our hands and we could feel her sending love. The she opened her eyes and gave us a beautiful, happy smile, squeezed our hands, and then . . . then she was gone." He was sobbing softly now.

"I wish I were there to hold you," I murmured. "Are you going to be all right?"

"I'll be okay. It's still new and raw. She was one helluva lady."

"How is Sylvia?"

"She's here — let me put her on."

"Daphne," was all she said through tears.

"I'm so sorry, Sylvia." *Inane, meaningless words!* "But she's at peace now."

"I hope so," she whispered. "God, we're going to miss her."

"I know. Is there anything I can do?"

"Nothing that I can think of. Vance may call you; I

gave him your number, just in case."

"That's fine. Have you decided when the funeral will be?" *Oh, wonderful, Daphne — all business when your two best friends are hurting!*

"No. We haven't done much but cry." She laughed shakily through her tears. "Trevor wants to talk to you again. Thanks for being there, Daphne. For both of us."

"Sylvia, remember I love both of you."

"And we love you. Here's Trevor."

He was more in control now. "Angel, I'm going to have to cancel the trip to Monte Carlo. Please forgive me, but we have to take care of her estate, get the house ready to sell. . . I'm not sure when we'll be back."

"Trevor my love, there's nothing to forgive. Our time can wait. You have more important things to do now."

"Maybe we can do Paris later. Or Rome."

"Stop worrying about it, please. I understand."

"I need you in my life, Daphne. I've become very aware of that lately."

"I'll be here. I promise. Do what you need to do and come home. I might even spring for Chinese carry-out."

I heard a ragged chuckle. "I'm holding you to that."

"What? Being here, or Chinese carry-out?"

"Both. Thanks for understanding."

"I love you both. Now go do what you have to do and call if you can."

He gave me phone numbers where I could reach them — maybe — and rang off.

ᔕ   ᔕ

It was several weeks before they got back to town, and I could see, by the time the four of us sat down for a quiet evening together, that the twins had come to terms with their loss. They both spoke tenderly of their grand-parents, laughing together about happy times from their childhood. It was good to see them laugh, but I regretted that I hadn't been able to be with them during the crisis.

"I thought a couple of times about flying down to lend my support," I told them. "But I knew I'd probably be in the way and you had things to get done."

"You'll never be in the way," Trevor replied firmly, tightening his arm around me for emphasis. "But there wouldn't have been a lot for you to do, and you had things here you needed to do. How did your sales calls go?"

"Better than I expected. I'm ashamed to admit that one woman said she had been interested in the Country Cuzzin line for some time, but assumed we were an exclusive house. We could have had the account three years ago if I hadn't been so complacent."

"Which reminds me," Vance put in. "Call this guy." He handed me a business card. "Lytle Builders is one of our subs, and they're considering doing some interior decoration. I doubt it'll turn into a huge account, but they're reliable and they do good work."

Long after Sylvia and Vance went to bed, Trevor and I sat, wrapped in each other's arms, enjoying the closeness and talking little. I kept thinking I should get home, but I couldn't quite pull myself out of the warmth of his arms. "It feels like ages since I've been in your arms," I murmured. "It feels so *right*."

"It *is* right," he blew into my hair and watched the effect with a satisfied smile. "Your hair is your best feature, did you know that? It's like it has a life of its own."

"It does, especially in the morning when I'm in a hurry. It's like a spoiled child, doing what *it* wants to do."

Trevor didn't speak for a long time, and I sensed he was struggling with something. I pulled away and looked at him. "What is it?"

He hesitated, staring at me with a puzzled expression. "Who are you?"

"What?"

"Who are you? Where did you come from? Why did

you wait so long to show up in my life? And how in god's name did I ever survive this long without you?"

"I come from forever," I teased. "Remember?"

But he wasn't in a joking mood. Mystified by his sudden seriousness, I waited.

Finally he spoke, his voice soft and his eyes far away. "I swore I'd never say this to a woman again, but will you marry me?"

"*What?*"

"Marriage. You know, till death do us part and all that stuff."

Panic seized me. I struggled for words. "Of all the things I've dreamed of your saying, this one never occurred to me. I thought you liked your independence."

"I do. I see no reason why we can't continue to be independent people. I just want you in my life, and I . . . I'm not sure I can put it into words, but, busy as we were with Mom's estate, thoughts of you kept intruding. Silly things, like wondering what it would be like to come home knowing you'd be there. Being able to snuggle down in bed without one of us having to get up and go home." He chuckled softly. "I even wondered what it would be like to have a fight with you and make up afterward."

He blew on my hair again, then buried his face in it, his arms tightening around me. "I don't want to lose you Daphne, but I don't want to clip your wings, either. And there's something tawdry about just living together. I want to do it right — and I don't want to touch you that way until it is right. Does that make any sense?"

Something inside me released — a barrier I didn't even know was there. For the first time in my life I understood what it felt like to be totally committed to someone. I had assumed we would eventually wind up living together; marriage had never occurred to me. Now it was the most natural thing in the world — the most *right* thing.

"Three hours ago, if you'd asked me the same question, I might have said you were out of your mind. I have no idea what just happened to me, Trevor West Elliot, but I would be honored to be your wife."

He pulled back, staring wide-eyed at me. "You mean that?"

"Yes. Don't you?"

His arms wrapped so tightly around me I could hardly breathe, Trevor whispered, "More than I ever meant anything in my life." Then he kissed me and the world went away again.

Much later he said softly, "I'm throwing you out, my beloved, because if you stay you'll be in danger."

I nodded and stood up, aware that I was still afraid of the dark side of me. But I also knew that, if he had made even one move in the direction of the bedroom, I would have happily followed him. He combed my hair with his fingers, smiling into my eyes. "God, you're beautiful." He kissed the tip of my nose. "Go home, seductress."

At the door he held me at arm's length, studying me as if he'd never seen me before. "How did I ever deserve such a delicious creature?"

"I guess you're a glutton for punishment," I teased. "Good night, my foolish love."

"Let's do it in Paris."

"Do what?"

"Get married. I know a Catholic priest there who'd be happy to perform the ceremony, and we'll spend a month in Europe. I can get some assignments and we can take a working vacation."

"Do you think Sylvia would allow that?"

He smiled ruefully. "No, you're probably right. Okay, we'll have the wedding here and honeymoon in Europe."

I kissed him. "It sounds wonderful, as long as it doesn't turn into a huge production. I'd like a small, private ceremony."

"You aren't going to change your mind, are you?" He

reminded me of a small boy, afraid I was going to take his new puppy from him.

"Not in a million years. We've apparently spent several lifetimes together. I should be able to tolerate one more with you. But after that I'm going to find someone else!"

He grinned. "It's a deal. I figure after ten or fifteen lives together we should be exploring other relationships anyhow. We don't want to get into a rut."

Realizing we were babbling to keep me from leaving, I kissed him gently. "I'm going home before you decide to rape me."

"Oh, I've already decided to do that. But I plan to have your full cooperation when I do."

11

Sylvia and Vance, delighted at our engagement, declared it should be a double wedding and the four of us,
like children anticipating Christmas, made outrageous
plans and abandoned them for more outrageous plans.
Trevor wanted a winter wedding on skis but agreed that
having to spend our honeymoon with me in the hospital with a broken leg wasn't worth the price. Finally we
settled on a small private ceremony with just a few close
friends and relatives. Sylvia and I decided to wear simple matching evening dresses that could be worn later
to parties.

Autumn was upon us before we knew it. Trevor had
been in and out of the country on assignments and,
much as I loved him, I admitted to him ruefully that it
was kind of nice to have my own life once in a while. I
expected him to be hurt; instead he grinned. "Good. I
want you to stay independent. The fact that we're married doesn't mean we have to be grafted to each other.
You have a business to run, I have trips to make. If we
can make them together occasionally, fine — but there

are going to be times when we'll be glad to get rid of each other, and that is as it should be."

He had one more assignment, in Bolivia, before the wedding. "Should be an easy one," he told me. "One of the oil companies wants some PR photos and write-ups to use in their annual report. I can do that with my eyes closed, but it's good money. They're even giving me an American sidekick to carry equipment and drive the jeep and run errands. The guy speaks Spanish, too, which will be a help."

"Why? You speak Spanish fluently."

"It's always nice to have a backup. I suspect, however, that he's really there to be sure I take the right pictures and talk to the right people."

"A minder?"

He grinned. "Yeah."

Something about this trip bothered me. "Be careful, Trevor."

He kissed the top of my head. "I always am. I'll be back before you know it. You're just suffering from pre-big-event jitters." Tilting my chin up he smiled into my eyes. "You aren't going to change your mind at the last minute, are you?"

"Are you kidding? And lose out on all that wealth you inherited from your grandmother?"

Trevor chuckled. "Thank god. I was afraid you might be marrying me for love. A financially driven marriage makes much more sense."

"I have no intention of telling you how much I love you; your ego's big enough as it is."

With Trevor out of the way for a few days, I threw myself into workaholic mode, watching in satisfaction as our receivables began to inch up again. LuAnne took over more of the dealing with suppliers and I concentrated on selling. I tried not to think about the wedding, for in spite of what I had told Trevor, I was indeed beginning to get the jitters. Memories of that hideous night and afternoon with Ron haunted me and I wondered if Trevor would be able to defend himself if I lost it completely. What does a man do on his wedding night when he discovers he's married an axe murderer?

Trevor admitted that while he was working, the rest of the world simply ceased to exist for him, so he seldom called when he was out of the country "I hope you can put up with that, Daphne. Don't expect anything from me except monosyllables until the assignment is finished." The first time I had felt slighted, but I soon saw the humor in it. That was the way Trevor Elliot was, and who was I to try to change it, especially since I did much the same thing? I simply stayed out of his way until he emerged from that other universe.

The day he was due to arrive home from Bolivia, I was restless and nervous. Assuming it was simply, as he put it, "pre-big-event jitters", I tried to find something to lose myself in. I went over my list of wedding invitations again, wondering if I'd missed someone, but I couldn't get interested. I tried to read a book but the words were meaningless. Music, normally so soothing to me, rasped on raw nerves. Everything irritated me, and as the evening dragged on I realized I was becoming increasingly, unreasonably angry. By the time the phone rang about ten o'clock, I was a rabid tiger trapped in a small cage.

When it turned out to be Sylvia and not Trevor, I had all I could do to keep from screaming at her. But my anger evaporated when I heard the tears in her voice.

"Trevor's been arrested."

"What? How? When?"

"I don't have any details. Jim, the guy Trevor was traveling with, just got back and called me. He said they arrested Trevor at the airport — claimed he was a spy. That's all he knows, because they hustled Jim onto the airplane and he had to leave Trevor there."

"Can't the company he was working for do any-thing?"

"They're trying, but of course this late at night no-body's available."

Suddenly I knew where my anger had come from. "Do you know what time this happened?"

"Sometime late this afternoon. Why?"

"Because that's about the time I started to feel a ris-ing tide of unreasonable anger. I think I sensed he was in danger."

She broke down then. "Oh, Daphne, I'm so scared!"

"Is Vance with you?"

"No, he's out of town until tomorrow."

"I'm coming over. I don't think either one of us should be alone tonight."

"Please, yes."

"Will you be all right until I get there?"

"Just hurry. Please."

"I'll see you in about thirty minutes."

I was icily calm as I made plans. No time for hyste-ria; that could come later. I called LuAnne and told her what had happened. "I may be out of pocket until this gets settled. Do you think you can handle things?"

"Of course. Don't worry about a thing. Have your phones transferred here for the night and I'll transfer them back tomorrow when I come into the office. That way if anyone calls there'll be somebody to answer and I can act as go-between. Just try to stay in touch as much as you can."

"I'll keep my cell phone on," I told her.

"God, I hope he's okay," LuAnne muttered.

"He is, so far."

"How do you know?"

"Because, strange as it may sound, I can feel him in my head, and we can communicate a little. He's scared but not in pain."

"It doesn't sound strange at all, not with the ties you two have."

"I'll be in touch."

❧   ❧

Through the long night Sylvia and I sat together, holding hands, waiting. We didn't even consider sleep. After an initial outburst of tears, Sylvia got herself more or less under control and we made hazy plans: embassies to call; maybe the State Department; people at Milltown Oil, the company that had commissioned Trevor.

The inactivity nearly drove me to a frenzy, but there was nothing to be done until offices opened in the morning. I got on the internet and learned as much as I could about Bolivia — although I had the strangest feeling that this had nothing whatsoever to do with Bolivia. Sylvia had the phone number for Jim Garcia, Trevor's traveling companion, and I called him as early as I dared.

"I don't know much," he told me. "We were at the gate, ready to board. I was ahead of Trevor in line, and they were making a final passport check. They checked mine and waved me through, but when they got to Trevor, there was something about his passport that caught their attention. I heard something about 'all those stamps,' and then somebody was shouting 'spy!' and they had him spread-eagled on the floor. I tried to go back but they barred my way and yelled at me to get on the plane. I tried to explain that we were together, and somebody threatened me with a gun. Jesus, they were carrying assault weapons! I thought the best thing for me to do was get back here and try to get some help."

"Can't the people at your company do anything?"

"I don't know. I've tried to call everybody I could think of, but nobody has any authority in a situation like this, and nobody seems to know how to get in touch with the president of the company."

"For god's sake, a man's life is in danger!"

"I know — I know. I'm doing the best I can. I'm going into the office now to try to get somebody's attention."

I gave him every phone number I could think of to reach me and made him promise to call as soon as he found somebody with some authority.

I hung up and tried to concentrate on Trevor, to send him love and hope. I thought I felt a flicker of response, but I couldn't be sure if it was just my imagination. I wished I knew more about this strange bond between us — and I tried not to think about what I'd do if they killed him.

Sylvia and I divided the list of phone numbers. She had the advantage of being his sister; I took the part of the list that we hoped wouldn't require an "official" relationship. But because we had so little information, we got pretty much nowhere. The logical side of me wasn't too surprised. How many calls must government agencies get every day from hysterical women claiming their boyfriends or husbands have absconded? All the conversations were variations on the same theme.

"Why was he arrested?"

"I don't know — they just grabbed him at the airport."

"What did he do to get arrested?"

"I don't know — as far as I know, nothing."

"Who arrested him?"

"I don't know. Soldiers. They were carrying assault weapons."

"Airport police?"

"I don't think so. According to the guy who was with him, they were dressed in military camo."

"What happened to the guy who was with him?"

"They forced him to get on the plane and come home alone."

"What were they doing in Bolivia?"

"Trevor's a photojournalist. He was on assignment there."

"What kind of assignment?"

"Public relations for Milltown Oil Company."

"Was he carrying a weapon?"

"Trevor? No!"

"Are you sure?"

"Well, no. . ." I'd never thought to ask him.

"I'd suggest you call back when you have more information."

At the end of an exhausting day, we had made no headway whatsoever. There was nothing on the news, and it was then that we began to suspect that Milltown Oil was going to hush the matter up. Late in the afternoon Jim Garcia called, nearly in tears, to say all he'd run into were stone walls. "They're not even acknowledging Trevor was working for them."

"What? They sent you down there with him!"

"Yeah, right. Well, according to the official bullshit, I was down there on my own and they've never heard of Trevor Elliot."

"But what did he *do*?" I demanded. "Was he taking pictures of the wrong things? Talking to the wrong people? Did he get in a fight or an argument? Why did they arrest him?"

"I wish to god I knew," Garcia answered. "Everything was perfectly fine, we had a great time, Trevor got some good pictures, there was a nice luncheon for us, and then we headed for the airport. We got through the first check-in just fine, no problems at all. We already had our boarding passes and they started this last-minute check. When they got to him, all hell broke loose." He hesitated. "You know, I got the impression they were looking for someone or something specific — that it was no routine check. I can't explain it, but that's the feeling I got."

"Is there any possibility at all that Trevor took pictures — even accidentally — of something he shouldn't have?"

Garcia thought for a moment. "I don't see how he could have. We were carefully monitored and we saw only what they wanted us to see. I remember Trevor grumbling about it privately to me, but he's enough of a professional to keep his mouth shut, and he didn't want to do anything that might jeopardize your marriage plans. He sure thinks a lot of you."

A clerk or whatever at the Bolivian embassy in Washington was sympathetic and promised to have someone call back. When no one had called within three hours, I called again, only to have another clerk assure me that the matter was being looked into and someone would call. The next day I tried again, demanding to talk to the ambassador himself. "I'm so sorry," another clerk said smoothly. "The ambassador is out of the country at the moment. But I'll have his deputy call as soon as we have some news."

A woman in our senator's office assured me that they would investigate immediately. At least she called back, only to say that there was no report of an American being arrested in Bolivia and unless we could get more facts or documentation of some sort, there was little they could do. But I was to call her immediately — she gave me her direct number — as soon as I had something.

A call to our embassy in Bolivia resulted in a great deal of sympathy and not much more.

A very kind young man at the state department assured me that the case would be looked into, "but I can't promise you anything, Ms. Morris. Unfortunately, incidents like this happen all too often, and Bolivia is one of the worst countries for kidnapping tourists. We simply don't have the manpower to track them all down."

"But he's not a tourist. He's a well-known photo-journalist; his work has appeared in major news publications."

"Then perhaps the publication he was working for may be able to help you."

"Unfortunately, he was on a freelance assignment.

The company he was working for refuses to accept responsibility. They claim he was there on his own and what he was doing for them was purely on speculation — in spite of the fact that they sent one of their representatives down there with him."

"I am sorry, Ms. Morris. Believe me, if I could do more, I would."

Three days passed in increasing frustration. Neither Sylvia nor I got much sleep. When I did sleep, I was haunted by violent dreams. Sometimes I was the victim, sometimes I was the perpetrator. The images were vague and confusing but they were always bloody. Once I dreamed Trevor had been shot and I woke up screaming.

Vance tried using some of his contacts in the government, to no avail. It was becoming increasingly apparent to all of us that, no matter how important Trevor West Elliot was to us, he was simply not important to anybody else.

Always in the back of my exhaustion-fogged mind was the feeling that there was more to this than there appeared to be. I'd lost track of the number of people I'd talked to — sometimes screamed at — but I remembered one person telling me that there was a possibility that Trevor was being held for ransom. "They may think he's affiliated with one of the big news companies like CNN or NBC, and believe the company will pay for his release."

I recalled Trevor's discussion about express kidnappings. "I'm afraid to ask what will happen when they realize that's not the case."

There was a long pause on the other end of the line. Then, "Please don't ask."

☙   ❧

The decision had been there all along, waiting patiently for me to acknowledge it. I raised my head and looked at Vance and Sylvia, slumped at the other end of the table. Sylvia, in an old shirt and jeans, hair hanging in her eyes, was doodling mindlessly on her pad of paper; Vance hadn't shaved in two days. Books and papers littered the floor and the table. Cartons of uneaten carry-out were shoved to one side. There were three broken pencils on my writing pad, evidence of the rising rage in me. "I can't take this anymore," I announced. "There's only one thing to do. I'm going down there."

"Where?" Sylvia asked muzzily.

"Bolivia."

She was instantly awake. "Daphne, you can't!"

"Why?"

"It's too dangerous!"

"Why should it be dangerous? I'm just going to ask some questions."

"And get yourself shot," Vance interjected. "Sylvia's right; we don't want to lose you, too."

"I don't think you understand. Without Trevor there is no reason for me to live. I can't simply sit here; I have to at least try. And what was it you said to me once, Sylvia? 'You are an intelligent, independent woman. You can make it on your own, and don't ever let anybody tell you otherwise!' "

"But what will you do?" she wailed. "How will you find him? There's apparently no official record of anything happening to him."

"I have no idea what I'll do. But I have business contacts in Bolivia and I think I still have an uncle or two in Peru. I look enough like my mother that I could pass for South American, and I'll just . . . play it by ear, I guess. But I can't sit here any longer listening to platitudes from people who don't give a damn. I have to at least try, or I could never live with myself."

"Give it a few more days, Daphne," Vance said.

"Maybe something will come up."

"And maybe in a few days Trevor will be dead, if he isn't already. I can't take that chance."

Sylvia and Vance looked at each other. Then Vance sighed and I got ready for another argument. Instead he reached for his checkbook and wrote me a check for $20,000. "For tax purposes, consider it a loan. If there's any of it left when you get home, you can give it back. If not, don't worry about it. And if I have to find more, I can do that, up to a point."

"Vance, are you out of your mind?" Sylvia demanded.

Exhausted and stunned, all I could say was, "You have no idea how much this means to me."

"Just find him," he replied.

12

LuAnne took my news with her usual calm. "I think it's what you need to do, whether it's the smartest thing or not. Bring him back, Daphne. Bring *both* of you back. And don't worry about things here."

I suspected my parents would not be quite so encouraging. I dialed their number reluctantly.

"Button! It's good to hear your voice!" I could picture Papá's grey eyes laughing through his bushy grey eyebrows as he called to Mamá to pick up the extension. He was a big man in his 60s, still full of life and energy, and had called me by his pet name "Button" since I was an infant.

"Daphne, I'm so glad you called," Mamá caroled. "You haven't given us the latest on that delicious young man you've been seeing."

"Trevor?"

There was a confused silence. "Who is Trevor?" Papá asked. "And what happened to Ron? I thought he was the love of your life."

Oh, lord, has it been that long since I talked to them?

I had avoided calling them because I didn't want them to pick up on my distress about my financial woes, and it hadn't even occurred to me to tell them about my forthcoming marriage to Trevor.

"Uh, well, Ron and I sort of parted company. He's moving back to Miami."

"Are you all right?" Mamá, as always acutely tuned to my emotional vibrations.

"Well, yes and no. I'm all right, but a friend of mine isn't." I hesitated, wishing I'd rehearsed what I was going to say to them.

"What's up, Button?"

I told them, leaving out the parts about past lives and those hideous scenes with Ron. ". . . and Trevor was due home Friday but we learned he's been uh . . . detained. We can't get any information whatsoever out of anybody. We've tried the State Department, embassies, everybody we could think of. If anybody knows anything — and I really don't think they do — they're not admitting it. We were supposed to have been married in a few weeks," I added lamely. Suddenly I felt like a little girl again, with skinned knees, lisping my tale of woe to Papá. I wanted to crawl into his arms and have him make all the bad mans go away.

"What does 'detained' mean, Daphne?" Mamá asked.

"Uh. . . well, apparently he's been arrested." I could hear Mamá gasp.

"Why didn't you tell us about this Trevor guy before?" Papá demanded.

"I fully intended to. Things happened so fast — and I've been having some problems with my business, too; everything just piled up."

"It sounds to me as if you've gotten tangled up with a real jerk," Papá replied. "Is he the reason for your financial troubles?"

"No!"

"Count your blessings that he's out of your life and call Ron and apologize."

"I can't do that, Papá. I love Trevor. And he's no jerk."

"He goes off for weeks without staying in touch and gets arrested but he's no jerk?" Mamá put in.

"Mamá, I think you'll understand this. The first time I met Trevor, it was as if we'd known each other for . . . for forever. The connection was so *strong*. I've never felt anything like that before, but I think it's the same feeling you had when you first met Papá. It scared me at first, but then we discovered we had shared many past lives, and it all began to make sense." I could hear Papá snort in derision. Although I knew Mamá's spiritual heritage was one that accepted past lives and spiritual connections as a given, Papá's Scandinavian insistence on logic and concrete proof had always been an area in which they agreed to disagree.

"Daphne, this guy is trouble from the word go," Papá said. "You hardly know him. He claims to be a photo-journalist, but you don't really know that. What else is he doing on those trips of his? He could have been smuggling drugs. They no doubt had very good reason for arresting him."

"Papá, he has had feature articles published in some big-name magazines, like *Time* and *Newsweek*. And there was a time when you took some pretty big risks yourself." There was silence at the other end of the line. Mamá, the only daughter in a Peruvian family of six sons, had been closely protected. Papá, in Peru working at an archaeological dig for his doctorate in anthropology, had fallen instantly and hopelessly in love with the diminutive student with the huge brown eyes and long black hair. He had quite literally stolen her away in the night, then faced her family with the accomplished fact of their marriage. Barely getting out of the confrontation alive, Papá left hastily for the safety of the United States with his stolen bride.

"Your mother wasn't a globetrotting ne'er-do-well,"

Papá replied coldly. "She was — is — the daughter of a well-educated and highly respected member of upper-class Peruvian society. I knew her family well — knew her background. You yourself admit you hardly know this guy."

"Oh, but you're wrong — I've known him for millennia." I could picture Papá rolling his eyes. "I *do* know him, Papá. I've spent a lot of time with him and his twin sister. They're good people — the best. They're both highly educated and he has a reputation for incisive reporting."

I heard Papá's snort of disbelief; Mamá sighed deeply. "Daphne, honey," she said softly, "you must think carefully about this. This man may be very charming and I can see where you might be attracted to him, but globe-trotting adventurers have a reputation for hard drinking and womanizing. Think about what life with him will be like. Do you think he'll change his ways after you're married? He goes off for weeks at a time now; do you really think he'll suddenly settle down and get a steady job after you're married?"

"Why, no, Mamá. I wouldn't dream of asking him to change. I like him the way he is."

"You *like* having him gone for weeks at a time?" she demanded. "That's not a marriage."

"It is to us," I replied lamely. I took a deep breath. "Look, this isn't getting us anywhere, and I need to make plans. We can discuss all this once I get back."

"Get back? From where?" Papá demanded.

"I'm . . . I'm going to Bolivia. To try to find out what happened to Trevor."

"What!?" Papá was incredulous.

"It's the only thing I can think of, Papá! We've tried everything else!"

"Who's 'we'?"

"Trevor's twin sister and her fiancé. I figure I look enough like Mamá that I could pass for Peruvian and maybe find out what an American couldn't," I added hurriedly.

"Daphne," Mamá interrupted. "Please listen to me a moment. You may have Peruvian hair and eyes, but make no mistake: you will immediately be spotted as a *gringa* — an American. You will stick out like a sore thumb. You'll never pass for a Peruvian."

"Why? Most Americans think I'm a foreigner."

"Yes, I know. It's very hard to explain, but they will know immediately that you are not one of them. You simply can't blend in."

I didn't entirely believe her; all I had to do was look in the mirror. "I can't see that I have any other choice," I murmured. "I can't desert him, not now. Not the way I feel about him. You'll meet him when we get back, and then you'll understand."

"What if you don't come back?" Mamá whispered.

"Of course I'll be back, Mamá. What I wanted to ask is, aren't some of your brothers still living in Peru? I was hoping they might be able to help somehow."

"Are you joking?" Papá asked.

"No, Papá, I'm not. I'm desperate."

"I haven't had much contact with my family since Evan and I left Peru over forty years ago, especially after my mother died," Mamá said. "She and I kept in touch, but I have no idea where my brothers are now or if they're still alive."

"In any case," Papá interrupted, "we certainly wouldn't embroil her relatives in this hare-brained scheme of yours. As your father I'm telling you to drop this matter and get on with your life. Find a decent man like Ron and settle down. This Elliot guy is nothing but trouble; I can feel it in my bones."

"I'm sorry. I love you, but I love him, too, and I have to do this."

I was about to hang up when Mamá said, "Then I'm going with you."

"Consuela!"

"I have to, Evan. She'll never succeed alone."

"I love you for offering, Mamá, but. . ."

"No! I absolutely forbid it!" Papá shouted. "Daphne, stop acting like a spoiled brat! You have a business to run, and you need to concentrate on getting it back on its feet! This is no time to be acting like a love-sick teenager!"

"*Te quiero*, Papá," I said softly and hung up, then put my head in my hands and sobbed. I'd never felt so alone in my life.

But Papá's words scared me. On the surface, he was right. I'd only known Trevor and Sylvia for about six months, although we'd met nearly a year ago. What, really, did I know about Trevor's assignments? What was he really doing when he wasn't snapping pictures and taking notes? What was he taking pictures *of*? He apparently made a good income — he and Sylvia had adjoining condos in a very nice section of town — but I had no idea how much photojournalists made. Was he augmenting his income somehow? He could have been running drugs or laundering money for all I knew. I'd never thought to ask, and Papá was right — I should know better than to get involved with someone I knew nothing about.

And yet I *did* know him — knew him the moment I first saw him. Would a jerk like the one my father imagined refuse to tumble me into bed without a marriage ceremony? I tried to remember if I'd ever caught Trevor in a lie — even a small one — and I couldn't. Both he and Sylvia seemed to be — were, I was sure of it — honest people who had been up-front about their lives and their foibles. And yet there was that joking comment he'd made to the minister at dinner that evening about running out of women. . .

I stared out the window, fighting that feeling of foreboding again. Maybe Papá was right. Maybe I should forget about Trevor, leave him to his own devices. Surely nobody could blame me for doing nothing. After all, what could a mere woman do in a foreign country? I didn't even know who had arrested him or why. Maybe he really was involved in something illegal. I probably would be better off without him, and maybe this was some sort of cosmic answer to my doubts.

But the thought of living the rest of my life without Trevor, never feeling again the warmth of his arms around me, never being able to touch him, hear his low voice . . . Always wondering *what if*, always comparing every other man to him. . .

"I don't have any choice," I whimpered. "Forgive me, Papá; I have no choice at all."

∂⟩ ⟨∂

Trevor had taught me the rudiments of meditation and I settled into a comfortable chair and closed my eyes, trying to relax every muscle and quiet my mind. It wasn't easy; my thoughts skittered all over the place — plans to make, packing to do, reservations to confirm, people to call (*remember to call Jim Garcia*), worries about Country Cuzzin — but gradually I slipped into a light trance, reaching out for Trevor's mind. I knew the "feel" of his mental touch now, and I opened myself to it. Finally I could feel a faint flicker, and I tried to "turn up the volume". Suddenly his presence was so real that I gasped and opened my eyes, half expecting to see him sitting next to me. I closed them again quickly to re-establish contact, feeling his gentle presence in my mind then, sending love and assurance. There were no words, but an overwhelming feeling of love, which I tried to send in return. "I'm coming, my beloved," I whispered. "Please hold on."

And then the contact was broken and I was alone in my darkened living room.

I glanced at my watch. Still early enough to call Jim Garcia.

"Wait a sec," he said. "Let me turn the TV down."

When he came back, I said, "Jim, I know we've been all over this before, but I need any information you might have forgotten — any scrap, anything you might have thought of since we last talked."

He thought for a moment. "I can't think of anything offhand. I take it you're not getting very far on your end?"

"No. I've decided the only thing to do is go down there."

"To Nu — to Bolivia?"

"Yes. Can you give me names of people I might contact down there — somebody with your company, officials, anybody? Even taxi drivers. I'm desperate."

He didn't say anything for a long time. Then he swore softly. At last he said, "Trevor made me promise I'd never tell you this, but we weren't in Bolivia. We flew into Bolivia and rented a jeep and driver for the rest of the way."

My father's warnings clanged in my head. "Where did you go, Jim?"

"Nueva Sangria."

"*What??*"

"Trevor figured you'd be upset if you knew. He said you'd talked about it and he had told you he'd never go back. He really loves you, Daphne." Garcia was talking fast now. "The rest of the assignment was exactly what he said it was. Milltown Oil is opening a plant in Nueva Sangria and they wanted pictures of rosy-cheeked workers laboring happily in the mills and oil fields. That's all we covered, and we did exactly as I told you before — took pictures of what they wanted, had lunch, and left for the airport in Bolivia."

"Where they arrested him."

Garcia sighed. "No. They stopped us before we

crossed the border. I think our driver was in on it, be-cause the soldiers grabbed Trevor and told us to drive on. I tried to protest but the driver gunned the motor and the last I saw of Trevor he was spread-eagled on the ground with six machine guns pointing at him. I'm guessing they wanted me to come home and tell people what happened — probably with the idea of ransom."

"Who arrested him, then?"

"Rebels, terrorists? I'm not sure. Everything hap-pened so fast. . ."

"Why in the hell didn't you tell someone about this?"

"I tried! God knows I tried — but nobody at Milltown Oil wanted to hear it. They're denying it even happened. Nobody wants to take the blame — especially with the civil situation as it is there."

"You mean they'll do nothing if they're contacted for ransom?"

"That's about the size of it."

"You goddam lying son of a bitch!" I screeched. "We've wasted nearly a week barking up all the wrong trees! Trevor could be dead by now!"

Garcia burst into tears. "I'm sorry! I'm so sorry! I didn't know what else to do! And my bosses made me swear to never tell anybody what happened."

My rage turned into icy control. "I want every name of every person you had any contact with whatsoever down there. Addresses and phone numbers if you have them. Maps, directions, descriptions — everything. I'm on my way over there now. You'd better start writing."

"But it's nearly ten o'clock!"

"Big fuckin' deal," I snarled. "I'll see you in twenty minutes, and you'd goddam well better open your door, or I'll scream my head off."

"I will, I will."

He must have been watching for me, because he opened the door just as I raised my hand to knock. His face was white, his hands trembling. He started to apologize again, but took one look at my face and shrank from me. "I'm on the computer now." He showed me into the bedroom where a computer sat amid a pile of papers and books, the monitor perched precariously on two stacks of paperbacks. "I'm doing a search through my notes, trying to find names and addresses. It should be enough to get you started."

I sat on the end of the unmade bed and waited impatiently, knowing if I spoke I'd start screaming at him — or worse. Struggling to contain the same rage I had felt that afternoon with Ron, I was afraid of myself.

We barely spoke for over an hour. Finally he handed me a printout of names, addresses, phone numbers, and some crudely-drawn maps.

"This is the main office." He pointed to a hand-drawn floor plan. "Diego Ventura's office is at the end of this hall. He's the manager of the plant — but he may have already been warned not to talk about this. He acted very friendly when we were there, but in those countries a guy can look you in the eye and smile while he stabs you in the gut. For god's sake, Daphne, be careful. This is no place for a woman alone."

I gave him an evil smile. "You coming with me?"

"I can't! They'll fire me if they find out I've even done this much."

"Where are Trevor's notes and equipment?"

"The company investigators confiscated everything. They even took my laptop. It's lucky I made remote on-line backups."

I moved toward the door. "Anything else you conveniently forgot?" I snarled.

"Look, I'm more sorry than I can possibly say. Trevor was a great guy — I never would have agreed to go on this trip if I'd known what was going to happen."

"What do you mean, '*was* a great guy'?"

"Well, it's just a figure of speech. I'm sure he'll be fine. It'll turn out to be a case of mistaken identity or something, and he'll be released soon."

I couldn't help it — I backhanded him across the face as hard as I could and slammed the door on his cry of pain.

There were six of them. They'd caught me hunting alone in the wilderness, far from my village. Now they circled like a pack of wolves, snarling and sniggering. One of them couldn't take his eyes off me. He stared at my blonde hair, then his eyes moved to my chest and he swallowed hard, his eyes wet and hungry, his jaw slack. Obviously he'd never seen a female of my race before. They were ugly little men, dark and stooped and hairy; I towered several hands above the tallest of them. They stank, too; I didn't have to get downwind to smell them. I wrinkled my nose in disgust.

They were obviously waiting for their leader to make the first move, and I could see he was worried about me, but his honor was at stake. I had a sword in one hand and my spear in the other, but the only weapons they carried were strange-looking little lances. The leader came at me then, low and fast. I feinted to the left and held my sword at an angle so he ran right into it — but he twisted just in time so it only grazed his shoulder, although he stumbled to his knees. Infuriated, he rose as another broke from the circle and rushed me. I lunged at him with my spear — missed — then sliced at a third with my sword. This time I connected, and he fell screaming to the ground, one arm nearly severed. The leader was moving again, and I waited until he was close, then caught his chin with the toe of my boot; it was laughably easy — he was so short. His head snapped back and he was down, his head at a funny angle. That left four, and they circled again, much more wary now. But I had managed to maneuver so my back was to a boulder. In a move I had practiced a thousand times, I dropped my sword and grabbed my knife, sending it winging through the air before they had time to react. It landed with a satisfyingly wet thuk *in the chest of the one nearest me. He fell to the ground screaming, his scream choked off by the blood flooding from his mouth. I had my sword back in my hand before the rest understood what had happened.*

The remaining three turned and ran, not even bothering to retrieve the one left alive.

I stood over him, watching with interest as the blood flowed from his arm. He was the one who had eyed me with such lust. He looked very young, but it was hard to tell with this alien little race. Tears of terror and pain in his eyes, he struggled to his knees and bowed his head, pleading for mercy. I dipped my fingers in his blood and smeared it on my face: one line under each eye, one across my forehead, another down my nose: honor-marks of battle. Then I licked my fingers; the taste was salty and metallic.

I laughed, and he raised his head in surprise. But my sword was already descending, and his head bounced to the ground. Retrieving my knife, I broke into an easy lope that would take me home long before dark.

I awoke with a gasp, but this time there were no tears, no fear. In the darkness of my twenty-first century bedroom, I knew what I had experienced, and suddenly I knew the transformation was complete. I felt no emotion whatsoever. I was the Woman of Ice and Snow—that had been my name in that lifetime. And Woman of Ice and Snow I would remain until Trevor was safe in my arms.

I climbed out of bed and stared at my reflection in the mirror. The person staring back was not me. The eyes were cold, hard, and calculating. The face was an icy mask. Even my posture was different, and as I eyed this strange apparition, an inner vow formed: I would find Trevor; I would bring him home. Nothing except death would stop me — and I realized I didn't care at all whether I lived or died. Nothing mattered except freeing Trevor.

That was what we had agreed to do in this lifetime, and the knowledge brought a sense of relief.

❧   ❧

At the airport, several people recoiled from the look on my face. Sylvia stared at me with a kind of horror. "Daphne, I don't even know you anymore. You've changed — and the change is scary."

"I have a job to do."

"For god's sake, please be careful."

"Don't worry; Trevor will come home."

"*Both* of you come home. Please."

I handed Sylvia a big brown envelope. "I hope you won't need these, but here are my will and a document giving you power of attorney. I left my share of Country Cuzzin to LuAnne. I don't think my parents will object, but if anything should happen to me, I hope you'll be sure LuAnne gets the whole company."

Then I nodded to Vance, who, sensing I wanted no physical contact, merely nodded in return and put his arm around Sylvia as I boarded the plane without a backward glance.

13

On the long flight I tried to memorize everything Jim Garcia had given me. I had to admit he had done a thorough job in the short time he'd had; I was looking at a sizeable book of downloads, documents and lists.

An article he'd found on a traveler's website gave me much of the background I needed.

Nueva Sangria had been carved out of the middle of South America during the Chaco War between Bolivia and Paraguay in the 1930s. Because it was low and marshy, neither of the two countries paid much attention when a group of semi-nomadic Indians banded together to claim a chunk of land about the size of Rhode Island as their own, calling it Nueva Sangria de Cristo.

Most of the natives spoke Spanish, but the local Indian dialect was Queterá, and the capital, Río Negro, was located near the site of an ancient temple complex which was being excavated by a consortium of anthropologists and archaeologists from the Universities of Pennsylvania and Florida. Some of their controversial finds challenged the accepted theory that Clovis man was the first human in the Americas.

"Hoo, boy, that's gonna upset the establishment," I muttered, remembering archaeological discussions with my father. As Trevor had said, Nueva Sangria's main export was the coca leaf, some of it for legitimate pharmaceutical purposes, most of it in various stages of its metamorphosis into cocaine.

But a large oil deposit had been discovered a little over a year ago, and suddenly there was a scramble among the superpowers to get in on the action. Confrontations between oil people — who wanted to destroy the coca fields and put in wells — and *cocaleros*, the coca farmers, were exacerbated by pressure from the U.S. and its allies to eradicate coca production altogether.

Trevor was right, I thought. *The place is a bomb waiting to go off. I just hope I can find him before somebody triggers it.*

The new government, theoretically set up as a democracy, soon deteriorated into a dictatorship. Calling himself *El Supremo,* the current president was rumored to be little more than a puppet of Generalissimo Manuel López, the leader of the Nueva Sangrian army, such as it was. But the *cocaleros* had organized a formidable underground army of their own, *El Ojo del Tigre*, The Eye of the Tiger. Like most covert organizations, it had attracted illegals and hangers-on: smugglers, thieves and desperados.

Jim Garcia had included an internet forum post from an Australian who had traveled extensively in Latin America. The writer flatly stated that Nueva Sangria was a police state run by a bunch of thugs who called themselves an army but were no match for the highly-disciplined and well-networked *El Ojo del Tigre*. Corruption was rife, and coca was as common as cigarettes and *chicha*, a powerful alcoholic beverage made from maize. "This is not a country for the faint of heart," the Australian wrote. "I'm a policeman and I was mugged and had my wallet stolen. Fortunately they were only interested in my money, because stories are common of tourists being robbed and beaten or killed. Under no circumstances should women — especially white women — travel alone in Nueva Sangria, as slave trafficking flourishes there. If they're too old or ugly for the brothels, they're forced to work in the coca fields." The writer also warned about express kidnapping, and I wondered again if my quest was really a need to perform some showy heroic feat — a fool's errand. But it was too late to turn back now. Fool I may be; I would find my beloved.

A small side note made me shudder: "The traveler should be aware that, due to the primitive conditions in Nueva Sangria, lice and fleas and the diseases they carry have reached almost epidemic proportions. Outbreaks of bubonic plague have been reported in many outlying areas. Symptoms appear in about three days, and include fever, lethargy, and swelling in the groin or armpit." *Bubonic plague? I thought that had been eradicated decades ago! Does insect repellent work on lice and fleas? I wonder if I can even buy something like that down there; it didn't occur to me to bring it with me.*

Other posts from the same website assured me that weapons of all kinds were easily obtainable in Nueva Sangria. "I saw AK-47s hawked on the streets like candy bars," one traveler commented. I found that both unnerving and reassuring. If I decided I needed a weapon, apparently obtaining one wouldn't be a problem.

As I studied — grateful that the plane wasn't full so I could spread my paperwork out and not have to chat with a curious seatmate — I felt the ice around my heart melt somewhat, as Daphne Morris began to reassert her presence. I smiled inwardly: *I should write a psychological thriller: The Many Faces of Daphne Morris.* At least I was doing something, taking action, instead of sitting helplessly in suburbia waiting for news of Trevor's death. For the first time in days, I allowed myself to relax somewhat, knowing it wouldn't last, knowing the Woman of Ice and Snow was waiting quietly in the shadows until I needed her again. And I would — I had no doubt of that.

I had been warned that delays and cancellations were the rule rather than the exception, but somebody's gods must have been smiling on me, for my connecting flight to Tarija left on time three hours after I landed in Santa Cruz. I've never been able to sleep on a plane, so by the time I landed at the airport in Tarija and got directions to José Sánchez's house, I had been awake for nearly 48 hours and hadn't eaten in eight. After a noisy argument with what I hoped was one of the honest taxi drivers, we agreed on a price and set off. Remembering Mamá's warning, I tried to be as imperious and demanding as I knew how, hinting at powerful friends and alluding to a weapon I supposedly carried.

José lived in what might charitably be called a sub-urb of Tarija. Although by U.S. standards his home was little more than a shack, by Latin American standards he was fairly well off. Located at the end of an unpaved street, the three-room adobe structure with thatched roof housed José, his wife and their six children, as well as various aunts, uncles, and cousins. Unlike many of the homes I saw, José's was neatly white-washed and the thatch was in good condition. The requisite wood-en bench sat outside the front door on a porch that ran the width of the house. An unpainted picket fence kept cows, goats and an assortment of chickens from stray-ing. There was even a TV antenna, although I didn't think there could be much to watch.

The three-year-old child who answered my knock took one look at me and ran screaming into the dark in-terior of the house. *Do I look that scary?* In a moment a woman came warily to the door. "Is this the home of José Sánchez?" I asked in Spanish, remembering to smile.

Her reply was in a language I didn't understand, but her sullen, suspicious expression was unmistakable.

"I am *Señora* Daphne Morris. *Señor* Sánchez sells his wood work through me." I spoke slowly, hoping that she would understand some of my words, in spite of my Peruvian accent.

She turned and shouted something unintelligible to someone in the house, but her eyes never left me. Eventually a man appeared, walking slowly with a cane. He was old and bent, but there was still a lively intelligence in his eyes.

"*Señor* Sánchez?"

"*Sí*. Who are you, please?"

"*Señora* Daphne Morris. I sell your furniture in North America. You know my agent, Victor González."

"*Señora* Dapnee Moreese?"

"Yes. . . *Sí*." José stared at me as if I were some sort of hallucination. "We met several years ago, remember? I came to Tarija when we first started doing business together." He nodded but said nothing. "Uh. . . may I come in? I'm afraid I need your help."

"Our home is very humble, *señora*, but you are welcome." The woman — I guessed it was his wife — sputtered an objection, but he ignored her and I moved carefully past her into the cool interior of the house. It was simply furnished — I suspected José had carved most of the furniture himself — but clean and neat. For some reason I was surprised; I had expected squalor.

José dismissed his wife with a jerk of his head, motioned me to a chair and sat heavily in one himself.

"You were not walking with a cane the last time I met you, *Señor* Sánchez," I commented.

He waved his hand dismissively. "It is nothing. I broke my leg a few years ago."

"It must make it difficult to get about."

"My son Carlos chooses the wood for me now. He is very good at it. One day he will take over my whole business."

There was a sudden silence, and I knew José was

politely waiting for me to explain my presence. I took a deep breath.

"*Señor* Sánchez, I know this is going to sound silly, but I need your help."

"My home is your home, *señora*," he replied gently.

As I told him about Trevor's dilemma, José listened intently, asking occasional questions. I fumbled frequently for the correct Spanish word, stopping to explain concepts I didn't have the word for. "We have been unable to get any help from our government," I concluded. "As far as I can tell, diplomatic relations are pretty much non-existent between the United States and Nueva Sangria."

He nodded. "I am not surprised. Things are very bad there. You should not go there, *señora*. Not even with a heavily armed guard."

"A guard would draw too much attention. I must do this quietly. I hope to be able to blend in enough that perhaps no one will realize my intent until it is too late."

I thought I saw a flash of amusement in his eyes, but all he said was, "How will you get into Nueva Sangria?"

"Honestly, I don't know. I thought you might have contacts there, someone who could help me get across the border, or who could at the very least offer some advice."

He thought for a moment, studying me carefully. "*Señora*, life and death come very cheaply there."

"I realize that. I see no other way. I can't leave him there to die. I . . . I love him very much."

He nodded. "One cannot deny the things of the heart."

"I will also need a weapon."

He looked up, surprised. "Can you use one?"

"Somewhat. I took a course in self-defense years ago. I'm hoping, frankly, to not have to use it except to wave it around and scare people."

"One who waves a gun around without intending to

use it is most dangerous to himself," José pointed out.

"Oh, I'll use it if I have to. But I'd rather use subterfuge."

"Forgive me if I speak too harshly, but you cannot go anywhere even in Bolivia dressed as you are. You are obviously a rich *gringa*, and an easy mark."

I nodded. "I was worried about the taxi ride here, but I had no choice."

"You took a taxi here alone?"

"Yes, from the airport. Why?"

"*Madre de Dios*, please do not do that again! It is very dangerous!"

"I tried to appear very sure of myself," I replied with a smile. José crossed himself and rolled his eyes. "Apparently it worked," I went on. "But I know you're right; I stick out like a sore thumb." The idiom didn't translate into Spanish, and I had to explain it.

José shouted something over his shoulder — the family apparently spoke one of the Indian dialects — and his wife reappeared, suspicious and resentful. He said something else to her and she looked me over carefully, then spat a reply. There was a sharp exchange and she shuffled out.

"I asked my wife to find some clothes for you. They will not fit you properly, but they will be less noticeable than what you are wearing."

"I will pay you for whatever expenses you incur," I said quickly.

The resentment in his eyes was instantaneous, and I hurried to make amends. "Please forgive me, *Señor* Sánchez; I did not intend to insult you. In our country it is customary to offer payment in such a situation. I know money is very scarce here, and I do not want to add to your burdens."

He nodded slightly, his expression softer. "It is the least I can do for a friend who has helped me to sell my furniture."

"There may be more expenses. Please — I beg of

you — you must let me know if something is beyond your means. It is not right that your children should go without food because of a stranger."

"But, *señora*, I told you — my house is yours."

I could see we weren't getting anywhere and I was relieved when his wife reappeared with a dress and sandals. The dress was old, but it was obviously her best dress. I took it from her gently and exclaimed over its beauty. Actually it was the ugliest thing I'd ever seen, but my praise had the desired effect, for her face lit up, even if she couldn't understand the words. I turned to José. "This dress is beautiful, but wouldn't it be best if I wore something less dressy?"

I apparently used the wrong word for "dressy," because I had to explain myself again. "I think I would be better off with some everyday clothes — even rags would be better. I know this must be her best dress, and I am deeply touched that she would offer it to a stranger, but I think I need something more . . . umm . . . everyday."

José spoke to her at length, and she nodded doubtfully. I held the dress to my heart briefly, miming that I loved it and wanted very much to keep it, then handed it back to her with a show of reluctance. The glow on her face told me I had made a friend.

The sandals — what I would call flip-flops — seemed to be the standard footwear, but hers were much too small for me. She stared at my feet in amazement and I had to smile: although I was about her height, my feet were almost half again as long as hers. She turned to her husband with a puzzled expression: *How can this be? A woman with a man's feet?* He said something to her and she nodded and left the room, returning a moment later with what I suspected were a pair of José's flip-flops and some old pants and a shirt, both satisfyingly ragged.

"Do women wear pants here?" I asked dubiously.

"Not many, but in the back country where you are going, people wear whatever they can find. You will be all right with these, and you can get a dress later if you need it.

Suddenly the room receded and I heard José call to me sharply from a long distance, "*Señora*, are you all right?"

"Uh. . . yes, I think so. I just realized I haven't slept for nearly two days."

"When did you last eat?"

"On the airplane to Santa Cruz."

He shouted something and a few minutes later a girl about eight years old brought *chipa* and *mate* — the local bread and tea. I hadn't had *chipa* since my last visit with my parents, and the first bite reminded me sharply of my last conversation with them. I shoved the pain aside. "You must sleep, *señora*," José said sternly. "Have you a place to stay?"

"Uh . . . no, I . . . I guess I didn't think that far. I came directly from the airport. I'm afraid I didn't plan this very well," I muttered. "I was so worried about Trevor. . ."

"You will stay here, of course. You must not go alone into the city. Our home is very poor, but you are welcome here."

"But you are already crowded." Although I had only seen four people, I could hear mutterings and rustlings of more from the other room, and I had seen many different sets of eyes peering around the corner at me. My Latin American agent, Victor, had told me that, like most homes in this country, José's was crowded with relatives. I really wanted a hot shower and a clean bed in a quiet hotel, but I knew anything resembling an American hotel would be miles from here, and I was too tired to even think of another taxi ride.

"There is always room for one more," José assured me. "But you must sleep now and the house is very busy." He thought for a moment. "If you would not be insulted, you could sleep in my workshop, which is separate from the house."

"But you need to be out there working."

"I am waiting for my son to bring wood for a special project and he will not return until late. In the meantime, you must sleep."

I didn't believe him, but, too exhausted to argue, I followed him out to the workshop, which was little more than a lean-to next to the cow shed. What I would have given for my nice comfortable bed at home! *I guess I'd better get used to roughing it*, I told myself, and stretched out gratefully on blankets on the dirt floor. I think I was asleep before I even lay down.

I came awake with a start, surrounded by brown-skinned people of all shapes, sizes and ages, staring at me solemnly in the dusky twilight. The eight-year-old girl I'd seen earlier carried a baby that was nearly a year old. The three-year-old who had answered the door picked his nose and eyed me thoughtfully. Somewhere a goat bleated, and flies buzzed in a small cloud around me. I smiled at a little girl near me and croaked, "Hello." My mouth was dry and I was too muzzy to remember the Spanish word. Startled, she scampered behind one of the adults and peered back at me. I moved carefully so as not to frighten the little crowd, but about that time José discovered my audience and shouted from the house. They moved back a few feet, and one of them called something to José. In a moment he appeared in the yard, shooing them away with his cane.

"I am sorry, *señora*. They have never seen a white woman before."

I smiled and sat up. "I was hoping to pass for a Peruvian," I told him ruefully.

He shook his head. "Please forgive me for speaking freely, *señora,* but you must understand this. Although your eyes and hair are dark, you are very obviously not from any of the South American countries. No matter where you go, no matter how you dress, you will immediately be recognized as a *gringa*."

"I was hoping nobody would even know I was here."

"In a small *barrio* like this, there are no secrets. Everybody already knows you're the *gringa* who sends me money sometimes."

❧   ❧

At dinner I was the center of attention, although communication with the family was non-verbal or through José. The meal was simple but satisfying, and the little ones watched my every move with huge eyes. José insisted on celebrating with a bottle of the local wine, a thin, vinegary red that was very powerful, especially as tired as I was. Throughout the evening neighbors came by to stare at the *gringa*, and I realized there was no hope of keeping my secret here. I could only hope the *barrio* telegraph didn't reach as far as the borders of Nueva Sangria.

After dinner José led me into the front room where several men stood, sat, or leaned against the walls. Their eyes were curious, but I detected hostility and a latent violence, and I was wary. For the first time it occurred to me how stupid I was to trust José, whom I knew only through Victor Gonzalez. José spoke for several minutes in the local dialect, gesturing occasionally, obviously explaining my predicament. When he came to the part that must have been about my determination to find Trevor, there were murmurs of astonishment and glances of new interest in my direction. A question and answer session followed, with José occasionally referring a question to me. Other than that, I sat without speaking, trying to appear very sure of myself, but I had to clasp my hands in my lap to hide the trembling. I had changed a great deal of money at the airport and I knew if they decided to kill me, I would be no match for this rough crowd. Several of them chewed on leaves which I suspected were coca, and I had no idea how irrational they might get.

José spoke to a couple of the men and they nodded and left. In rising panic, I wondered if they were going to get reinforcements. I was too tired to realize that these men would need no reinforcements if they decided to overpower me.

Finally José turned to me. "My son Carlos will guide you to the border. He has a friend in Nueva Sangria that he thinks might be willing to help, but it might cost you some money."

I hesitated, then decided on deception. "I have very little money, *Señor* Sánchez. I know Latin Americans think all *gringos* are rich, but I'm not. I spent nearly all I had on the airplane ticket down here. It might be best if I just tried to get in on my own."

"You cannot do that, *señora*! It is impossible, especially without the proper papers."

"But if I have no money, I have no choice, do I?"

There was a discussion among the men, and several of them left in obvious disgust. Only Carlos and two other men remained. Carlos spoke to me then, in Spanish. "This *gringo* you look for — you know where he is?"

"No. Only that he was arrested at the border near Ciudad Libre."

"You do not know where they take him?"

"No."

Carlos spoke to the other men and one of them rolled his eyes and muttered something. The other one snickered and Carlos turned back to me. "We have heard of such a one. I do not know if it is the same man, but he makes. . ." Lacking the right word, he held his hands in front of his face, miming holding a camera, and made clicking noises.

"Yes, he's a *fotógrafo*—a photographer. He takes pictures." I repeated the camera motion. "Do you know where he is? Is he all right?"

One of the men mumbled something, and there was

a general nod of agreement.

"We believe he is in the prison in Río Negro," José told me.

"How far is that?"

"A day to the border, another half day to Río Negro."

I groaned. Another two days wasted. Would Trevor be alive if I ever found him at all? And if he was, would he still be capable of travel? "Can we leave tonight?"

José spoke softly. "We must make plans tonight, *señora*, and you cannot cross the border in the daylight, for if you have no papers you will be refused — or arrested. If you leave at dawn, you will arrive at the border soon after the sun sets."

"*Señor* Sánchez," I hesitated. "Can they get me a weapon?"

Carlos spoke a few words to two men who had remained. They glanced at me in surprise, nodded and left.

Then Carlos turned to me with a little bow and said, "I will see you tomorrow, *señora*. Sleep well tonight, for we have a long way to go tomorrow." Then he was gone and I stared across the room at José.

"Are you afraid, *señora*?"

"A little. Mostly I'm afraid for Trevor. What if he's not even alive?"

José nodded. "That is possible, *señora*. Only the good God knows that, but you must put your faith in your own heart, for if God guides you truly, He will guide you well."

❧   ❦

Somewhat to my surprise, I slept well that night, rising with the rest of the family before dawn. José led me to his workshop where several handguns and knives had appeared. "Choose what you need, *señora*."

"My friend — please — I must be allowed to pay for these."

He shook his head. "If you come back, then you pay."

I chose a semi-automatic that felt right in my hand and had plenty of ammunition. I also chose two knives, one to wear at my belt and another with a wrist sheath. José tried to hide a supercilious smile. "You know how to use these, *señora*?" Without thinking, I spun and hurled the larger knife, burying it in the far wall, then pulled the gun, aiming at the knife with both hands before my imaginary assailant could move. My arms trembled as I stared through the gun sight at the knife vibrating in the wall. *How the hell did I do that?*

José nodded and said simply, "I hope you do as well with a real *bandido*, *señora*."

You and me both, my friend.

Carlos didn't arrive until well after sunrise. Picking at my food, I tried to hide my irritation as he chatted with his father over a light meal. By the time he finally turned to me, I was ready to scream with impatience.

José took my hands in his and stared into my eyes, a deep sorrow in his own. "*Vaya con dios, señora.* Go with God."

"Thank you, *señor*, for everything. I'll see you in a few days."

He seemed about to say something, then merely nodded and handed me my shoulder pack. I thought I saw tears in his eyes.

The entire neighborhood turned out to stare at us as we passed. Carlos was a handsome young man, probably about 20, and obviously popular in the community. A few called to him in the local dialect, and, judging by the coarse laughter, some of the comments were ribald. I was relieved when we reached the outskirts of town.

It was the first time I'd seen the open savannah from the ground. I remembered from Jim Garcia's notes that the area used to be heavily forested, but had been completely cleared and was now nothing but scrub trees and flat plains stretching to the visible horizon. It was barren and forbidding. Far behind us the mountains raised snowy, imperious heads to the sky.

The weather had been pleasant enough yesterday, but now, away from shade trees, the sun's heat was oppressive. I was glad I had decided to wear my own running shoes, for the flip-flops in my shoulder pack would never have been adequate. Carlos set a comfortable pace, urging me to stay close to him. Other than that, he spoke little — but I soon suspected he made this trip frequently, for I noticed he knew exactly where he was going, and he kept careful watch, alert to every telltale noise or signal. Finally I asked him about it.

"This is not a good place, *señora*," he answered. "Many bandits roam the lowlands, and farmers are wary of strangers. If we are stopped, you are my cousin. You have found work in Nueva Sangria and I am taking you there. You will stay with another cousin in Río Negro. Her husband runs a small hotel and restaurant there."

"Do you really have a cousin in Río Negro?"

"She is a distant cousin, but, yes."

"If I am your cousin," I said with a smile, "perhaps you should not call me *señora*." Carlos glanced at me hesitatingly. "Call me Consuela. Consuela de la Rosa. It was my mother's name."

He shook his head. "De la Rosa is a very well-known and respected name. You must use another. Consuela Rodríguez."

I repeated it aloud several times, and kept repeating it in my head as we walked.

The day — and the heat — progressed. My ragged shirt was soaked with perspiration, but Carlos' shirt wasn't even damp. Sometime around noon we stopped for a snack and he checked my water supply with dismay. "I guess I'd better try to ration it," I said ruefully. "I didn't realize how devastating the heat would be."

Motioning for me to wait, he disappeared into the brush. A few minutes later he was back, chewing on something. He handed me some smooth narrow green leaves. "Chew slowly and spit out what is left," he told me.

"That's coca, isn't it?"

He nodded.

I hesitated. "I think I would rather not, thank you."

Carlos looked at me in surprise. "Why? It is good for you."

I remembered Trevor's little discourse about coca not being addictive until it was processed into cocaine, but still I hesitated. "Won't it make me — " I searched for the right Spanish word — "drunk?" Was he hoping to get me so stoned he could overpower me and leave me alone in a *barranca* to die?

He laughed, and already I could see a change in him — but it was slight, and not particularly frightening. He appeared calmer, more at ease, more sure of himself, but not dangerously so. "It will make you feel better, *señora*, that is all. It will give you strength and help with the thirst." He shoved a leaf into my hand. "Try just a little."

I nibbled part of one leaf. The taste was bitter and unpleasant — but strangely familiar. "I don't feel anything," I said after a few minutes.

He grinned. "You did not try a big enough piece. Put the rest of the leaf in your mouth, and give it a little more time to work."

Actually, even that tiny piece did have an effect, although it was so minor I wouldn't have noticed if I hadn't been looking for it. My stomach seemed to settle down a bit for the first time in days. Reluctantly I put the whole leaf in my mouth and chewed. Carlos nodded and offered me a handful of the leaves. "When you have sucked all the juice out of that leaf, spit it out and take another."

"How many should I take at a time?"

"You will know when you have had enough." He watched me closely as I put two more leaves in my mouth, biting off the stems as he showed me.

The effect was gradual, but unmistakable. I couldn't put my finger on it, but I felt better, as if I'd had a strong jolt of caffeine without the jitters. The sun didn't feel quite so oppressive, and I wasn't as thirsty. Carlos nodded in satisfaction and we set off again. I hoped Trevor was right about coca not being addictive in this state.

Early in the afternoon we came to a dirt road — little more than a cart track — which Carlos said was the main highway into Río Negro, the capital of Nueva Sangria. Dust rose in nervous eddies and turned the grass and trees grey, but walking on the road was certainly easier than trudging through the brush. We had only gone a dozen yards when we heard a truck approaching from behind. Carlos pulled me out of sight behind some bushes, but when the truck came into view, he stepped out and waved. The decrepit Ford flatbed, which would have long ago been in a junk yard in the U.S., was piled high with boxes, parcels, and people. I wondered how it stayed in one piece, for it looked as if it was built entirely of rust and baling wire. Chickens cackled from a crate lashed to the top of the cab, and I thought I heard a goat. Carlos spoke briefly with the driver, then motioned for me to join him. "He says we can ride as far as the border. I told him my cousin is from the city and not used to walking."

That was true enough, but I eyed the truck dubiously. "There isn't room," I objected.

"There is always room. Come."

I still don't know how we managed, but the peasants cheerfully made room for two more on top of all the parcels, and we set off with a lurch. There was nothing to hold on to, and I nearly slid off when the truck started up. Laughing, they pulled me back as we careened down the road. Wedged between Carlos and a nearly-toothless old woman who needed a bath, I noticed that everyone was chewing coca leaves, but the sullenness usually associated with the consumption of alcohol or drugs was not in evidence. Indeed, everyone was having a wonderful time — and I realized I was, too. *American businesswoman goes native.*

I grinned as I clung to Carlos to keep from sliding off again. Deliberately I kept my mind off Trevor, knowing my fears for him would distract me. I must, for now, play the cheerful *Latina* traveling happily with her cousin. But I couldn't resist: just for a moment, I reached out a tendril of my mind to Trevor, hoping he'd sense my love and not what I was up to. I thought I felt a tender reply, but it could have been my imagination.

It was apparent the peasants were curious about me, for Carlos was kept busy answering questions. I recalled my mother's and José's warnings about my not blending in, and I wondered what Carlos was really telling them about me. But as truck lumbered through the afternoon heat, I realized I was beginning to understand a few words here and there, although Queterá, the Indian dialect they spoke, was entirely unfamiliar to me. Then I noticed the scenery looked vaguely familiar, too. But I'd never been south of Tarija before. On the other hand, lowlands look pretty much the same all over the world.

Someone started to sing, and the rest joined in. I thought I recognized the tune — perhaps it was one my mother had sung when I was a child. Mechanically I put another coca leaf in my mouth, and gazed out across the landscape. Stunted trees and brush languished in the heat. Dust rose in clouds behind the truck, covering everything — including the passengers — with a brownish-yellow coat.

Carlos leaned toward me. "Are you all right, *señora* — Consuela?"

"What? Oh, yes, I'm fine. Why?"

"You look very pale and far away. Perhaps the coca does not agree with you?"

"Just worried, I guess."

Two old men nudged each other, and, grinning, one of them muttered doubts about my being Carlos' cousin. I glared at him — and then realized I had understood what he said. Could coca leaves do that? What other explanation was there?

14

The truck jounced and the people around me laughed and chattered, the chickens squawking a crazy counterpoint. But suddenly I was somewhere else.

⋘ ⋙

It was just after sunset, and I was a small brown boy, almost black from the sun. My bare feet ached from squatting in a cold stream that ran through a cave formed by fallen trees. I could hear my brothers calling as they searched for me, and I giggled softly. They were far upwind; they wouldn't hear me. The cave stank of animal droppings and I could hear the rustling of mice or rats, but I would be gone long before they worked up the courage to come near me.

I was meeting my friend Dominique to explore the ancient ruins together. Tonight the moon would be full, and I quivered with anticipation. But I was not afraid — just excited, of course. My mother would be worried, but she always worried, and I was almost a man now — almost ten years old! — I could take care of myself. I knew when I got back she would cry and hold me close and make me promise never to frighten her like that again. And I would solemnly promise and be very sorry I had worried her. Until the next time. I liked being the spoiled youngest child, but nobody understood that I was old enough to take care of myself.

Footsteps! I crouched back farther into the cave and held my breath. "Leave him, if he wants to be left," my oldest brother Raul growled, his voice deliberately loud. "I'm tired of trying to keep track of him. Let him get eaten by a mountain lion if that's what he wants." They passed directly in front of the cave — I could see their bare feet raise little swirls of dust in the fading light. I knew my brother meant for me to hear his words, hoping to scare me out of hiding. I hadn't thought of mountain lions, and the silence left by my brothers' fading steps filled me with lonely terror. I nearly ran after them — had even taken a few cautious steps toward the cave mouth — when I remembered I'm almost a man. I can take care of myself. No mountain lion is going to frighten Juanito Maria Alvarez!

Shivering — from the cold water on my feet, of course! — I waited for Dominique. Where was he? He'd said he'd meet me at sunset! The night seemed to throb with danger.

Suddenly I heard a rustling in the brush — something huge. A mountain lion coming to drink before hunting? Would I be his first meal? I tried to push farther back into the cave, but it was little more than a shallow dent in the debris and my back was already to the wall. I couldn't get rid of the mental image of a huge cat lapping at the water, then catching my scent. I imagined the sharp claws reaching for me, heard the throaty hunter's snarl. I felt the cat's hot breath on my face and the long teeth rip at my throat, cutting off my screams. I saw my brothers the next morning finding my torn and bloody clothing and what was left of my *body. Raul, pretending he didn't care while he swallowed tears, saying, "He got what he deserved," but wishing he'd searched a little harder, a little longer.*

Swallowing a whimper, trying not to breathe, I prayed every prayer my mother had taught me. I wasn't sure the Blessed Virgin would answer the prayers of a naughty little boy, but I prayed anyhow, promising I would never — ever — be bad again if She would get me home safely tonight.

It was dark beyond the mouth of the cave now and I could hear the monster moving again. I clamped my jaw shut to keep from screaming. Suddenly a shadow fell across the entrance, blotting out the faint glow of the stars. My lungs quit working and I almost pissed myself in terror. The intruder moved closer; I could hear its heavy breathing. I tried to melt into the back of the cave.

"Juanito? Are you here?" Dominique! Weak with relief, I had to unlock frozen muscles before I could move. "Juanito! Where are you?"

Dominique jumped and yelped as I crawled out of the cave. "I'm right here!" I whispered hoarsely. "Don't make so much noise!"

"You scared me."

"Don't be such a baby." After all, I knew I was brave — I had just faced down a mountain lion — but I was glad it was too dark for Dominique to see I was trembling. "Let's go."

We had explored the ancient ruins of the temple near our village several times before, but always in the daylight. Tonight we had agreed to confront the ghosts we had heard so many stories about: the priest with a huge spear and no head, the young boy who had supposedly been sacrificed to the gods, the strange weeping noises one heard only at night. Dominique looked around uncertainly. "I don't know. . ."

"Don't tell me you're scared," I sneered.

"Of course not! I just. . . well, I don't feel so good. I think I ate something that made me sick."

"You're scared!"

"I am not!"

"Maybe we'd better do this some other night, then. I don't want you getting sick or passing out on me," *I said scornfully — and almost collapsed with relief when Dominique replied, with a great show of reluctance, "Maybe you're right."*

"You want me to walk home with you? You don't look so good." *Dominique nodded and I took his arm, hoping he couldn't tell I was trembling. We hurried through the woods, trying not to jump when we heard scary rustlings and cracklings in the brush. At first we joked about it, but the mood soon evaporated. Trees loomed like giants; underbrush grabbed at our ankles. Somewhere a big animal snuffled and a wildcat snarled. We were both trembling by the time we reached the village.*

At Dominique's door I grabbed his shoulder. "Let's keep this a secret," I whispered. "I won't say I was with you if you won't say you were with me."

Dominique nodded and slipped inside as I turned toward my own home. Even Mamá's tears were welcome that night, but I brushed her aside. "I'm fine, Mamá. I was fishing on the river and didn't realize how far I'd walked. I had to walk home in the dark, but I can take care of myself. I'm almost a man now, you know."

⅌   ⅍

Someone was shaking my arm. "Consuela! Are you all right?"

It was Carlos. With an effort, I focused on his face. "Yes, I'm fine."

"You passed out." He searched my face anxiously. "Are you sure you're fine? You were moaning."

"I guess the motion of the truck made me sleepy. I'm okay, really." I glanced around at the rest of the passengers, all staring at me with concern and curiosity.

Carlos leaned close and murmured in my ear, "We must walk the rest of the way. The truck will be searched when it crosses the border, and if they find the weapons we carry we endanger the others. Are you able to walk?" I nodded, still lost somewhere between the past and the present, and Carlos pounded on the cab of the truck. It lurched to a stop and he helped me climb down. The other passengers waved as the truck pulled away and the two old men grinned knowingly and nudged each other.

I looked around, no longer surprised that I recognized some landmarks. "How far is it to the border?" I asked.

"We are very near it," Carlos replied. "We must use the rest of the daylight to find a place to hide until we can cross safely after dark."

"Don't we have to cross a river?"

"*Sí*, the Río Negro. It forms the northern border of Nueva Sangria and gives the capital its name. We should be able to cross a few miles downriver, but we will have to leave the highway."

"Where are the ruins of the temple complex?" I didn't know how far Dominique and I had walked that night — fear had made our walk seem like hours. I wondered if the village still existed — or if it was now the city of Río Negro; I wasn't sure when that lifetime as Dominique had taken place.

"How do you know about the ruins?"

I shrugged. "They were mentioned in a brochure. My father's an archaeologist." I had to use the English word; I couldn't remember the Spanish one. Seeing his confusion, I added, "Someone who digs in and studies ancient ruins. I don't know the Spanish word."

He nodded. "I do not know the word, either, but I know what you mean. There are many people there —

gringos. The digging place is all fenced off and people dig with little shovels in little squares in the ground." His eyes flashed with anger. "They steal the treasures of our ancestors!"

I didn't think this was a good time to argue that most archaeologists these days were careful to turn true treasures over to the local ruling government; I doubted Carlos would understand the finer points.

But an idea had begun to form. "The ruins are not far from the city, are they?" I asked.

"An hour's walk. It is not far by truck."

"And they're between the river and the city?"

"*Sí*." He studied me for a moment, questions in his eyes, but when I said nothing more, he lead the way off the track, headed, as far as I could tell, west. It was near sunset when Carlos motioned for me to hide among some rocks and wait while he explored the path to the river. Glad to be off my feet for a while, I slipped out of my shoulder pack and took a cautious sip of water from my bottle. I didn't think there would be an opportunity to replenish it until I got to the city.

Suddenly my yearning for Trevor was a physical pain. I wanted desperately to feel his warm arms around me, and I feared that, in spite of my efforts, I'd never see him again. I pictured him a bloody corpse dangling from a stake, his body riddled with bullets. Tears slid down my cheeks. Although I suspected it wasn't a good idea, I closed my eyes and tried to relax my aching muscles and weary mind as I reached out for Trevor, calling his name softly in my mind. The strength of his response nearly knocked me over. It was that same feeling of vastness, of immense power, that I had experienced the first time I'd seen him. And through the vastness came a gentle whisper: *Cara mia, remember I love you.*

Wait for me, my love, I replied mentally. *I'm coming to you.*

There were no words, but I thought I felt a jolt of

surprise in reply.

I jumped as Carlos slid down the rock beside me. I was amazed that it was almost dark. He must have been gone over an hour. Apparently I had fallen asleep — had I dreamed the contact with Trevor?

"Are you all right, *señora*?"

"Consuela. Why do you keep asking me that?" I replied irritably. "I'm fine. Just tired. I'm not used to all this walking."

"Are you able to walk farther?"

I nodded. "I fell asleep, that's all."

Pointing, he said, "The river gets wider that way, but there is a way to cross. We will wait here until it is very dark, then cross downriver and walk back to the road." I nodded again, still lost somewhere between two worlds. "If you can go back to sleep, it would be well," he continued, studying me. "We still have a long way to go."

"I don't think I'll be able to go back to sleep, but I can keep watch while you do."

He hesitated, then nodded and made himself comfortable. Within minutes he was snoring softly.

I remembered Trevor talking about deliberately exploring past lives, but I'd never tried it. Suddenly I decided I'd find out what my arrogant little brown other self could teach me about his life and neighborhood. Moving quietly so as not to wake Carlos, I made myself as comfortable as I could against the rock — still warm from the day's heat — and closed my eyes again, picturing the cave where I had first encountered Juanito, reaching out to him with my mind as I had reached out to Trevor. I had no idea whether this was the way to do it, but it was worth a try.

With a jolt I found myself standing near a river, staring through Juanito's eyes across the muddy wa-

*ter. My fishing line was in my hand, but I wasn't inter-
ested in fishing, for on the opposite bank Estrellita was
running toward me, laughing and waving, her hair flying. I couldn't take my eyes off her breasts, bouncing
and jiggling beneath her thin blouse as she ran. I was
older this time, in my early teens, and volcanoes of hot
hormones thundered in my blood. I should have gone
downstream to the bridge, but I was too impatient.
Quickly I slipped down the bank and swam across
the river. The current was cold and swift from spring
runoff in the mountains, and twice I was pulled under
before I finally gained the opposite bank and dropped,
gasping, at Estrellita's feet.*

*"Oh, Juanito, what a lovely fool you are," she
crooned. "You nearly drowned." She knelt and pulled
my head into my lap.*

*I could smell the womanly scent of her. Her breasts
were inches from my face, and a delicious agony con-
sumed me. I smiled up at her. "It was worth it to be with
you." To my embarrassment, my voice broke, turning
my gallant compliment into a little boy's foolishness.
I knew my brothers had all gone through this phase,
but it didn't make it any less embarrassing. Estrellita
pretended not to notice, gently combing my wet hair
with her fingers My heart pounded, and I hoped she
wouldn't notice the swelling in my groin.*

*"How did you get away?" I asked when I could
make my throat work again.*

*"Mamá is not well today, and Papá and my broth-
er are working in the fields. When Mamá fell asleep, I
slipped out."*

"What if she wakes up?"

*Estrellita shrugged. "I will tell her I went out to pick
some flowers for her." Tears welled into her eyes and
she turned away, her hair a dark curtain to hide her
face. We both knew Estrellita's mother was dying, although nobody actually said so. Over the past months*

she had gradually wasted away, until she was little more than a skeleton, skin stretched tight across wasted bones. As frail as she was, I could still see the beauty there — beauty Estrellita had inherited.

I gently brushed the tears from her cheek. "Don't cry, Estrellita. It's such a lovely day, no time for tears."

She nodded, and I marveled at her ability to switch moods, for suddenly she laughed. "You're right, Juanito. Let's walk. I can't stay long."

I took her hand timidly and was rewarded with a shy smile. I was acutely aware of the heat and softness of her small hand in mine. We followed the river almost to the bridge, then sat on some rocks and talked. I guess we had heard the voice calling for quite some time before it registered. "It's Alvaro! Oh, Juanito, my brother must not see us together!"

"I'm not afraid of him."

"But I am! Hide, please, Juanito!" She kissed me quickly on the cheek and, my head roaring — she had never kissed me before — I ducked between some rocks.

I could hear Alvaro's angry voice and Estrellita's defiant reply. But when I heard the blow, I could not control my rage. He was looming over her, one huge hand bruising her arm, the other raised to slap her again. I hit his knees at a run, bowling him over, knocking Estrellita off her feet, too. He came up swinging and I lurched out of his reach. "Run, Estrellita!" I shouted. I didn't think he would hit her in front of their parents — if I could keep him here until she got home. She was on her feet and racing homeward as he started for me again, but I was smaller and faster. I hoped I could stay out of his reach, because I knew he'd kill me if he got his huge hands on me.

He lunged for my throat and I ducked and aimed a foot at his groin — a mistake. It only made him angrier and he came at me with a roar. I sidestepped and tripped him, then ran for the river. If I could get across before he did, there was a chance I could rally my brothers — and if he chased me all the way across the bridge, it would give Estrellita plenty of time to get home.

I ran so fast I felt I was flying, but I could hear him thundering behind me and I knew I couldn't make the bridge in time. Just as he grabbed for me, I dove off the bank, hit the river and started swimming, terror giving me speed and strength. But the current was danger-ously swift here and suddenly I was swimming for my life. Rocks loomed above me, whitewater boiled around them. Desperately I pushed away from one rock, but it was slippery and I caromed into another one. I gasped for breath and swallowed water as I plunged over a submerged rock and slammed into something hard.

Raul pounded me on the back again, bellowing, "Wake up, damn you! I'm not going to let you die! Spit it out!" I vomited water and took a deep breath. He sat back and stared at me, his eyes still hollow with fear. "Little brother, you will be the death of me yet. What in the name of the Blessed Virgin were you doing in the river?" His hair and clothes were still streaming with water, but I had no recollection of his pulling me out.

"I uh. . . slipped."

He eyed me sternly. "From which side of the river?"

"This one. Why?"

"Why was Alvaro standing on the opposite bank screaming?"

I shrugged. "How do I know?"

"You weren't with that girl again, were you?"

"What girl?"

"You know damn well what girl! You've been told to stay away from her! Papá has told you, her father has told you! What in the blessed name of the Virgin are you trying to do? Get yourself killed? You know what her brother's like!"

I burst into tears. "He was hitting her, Raul! He was going to hit her again! I didn't even think! I hit . . ." Suddenly I realized what I had said.

Raul stared at me, aghast. "You attacked Alvaro? All by yourself? Are you out of your goddam mind?"

"I couldn't help it," I said defiantly. "He was going to hit her again, and I went crazy."

"Little brother, do you think you've solved anything?" he asked me softly. "Do you really think he'll stop hurting her because you hit him once?"

"It was the only thing I could think of," I sobbed. "I had to stop him, if only that one time."

Raul sighed and shook his head, putting his arm around my shoulders. "Let's go home, Juanito."

❧   ❧

I pulled out of the trance with a gasp and glanced at Carlos, still sleeping peacefully, then sat back and thought over my dream — vision? By now, I was fairly used to recognizing people from this life in my other lives, but it still unnerved me a bit, especially this one — for Estrellita of the laughing eyes was Sylvia in this life. The idea that I would be physically attracted to Trevor's sister was distressing to say the least, and I wondered guiltily what Trevor — or Sylvia, for that matter — would say. I felt my face burn with embarrassment, although I suspected they both had run into similar situations in their explorations of past lives.

I stared around me, and realized the rock formation Juanito had hidden in was the very place Carlos and I hid in now. I shivered. *There's a reason for all this,* I told myself. *I don't believe I would have been led this far if there weren't some way to get Trevor out. I've got to keep telling myself that. I can't give in to fear. Oh, Trevor, hold on! I'm coming!*

15

A distant owl hooted and it began to rain heavily as Carlos led me down a steep path to the river. The crossing was little more than rocks and tree limbs scattered between the banks — I was fairly sure there had been a bridge here long ago — but the river foamed and thundered around the rocks. I wavered, my stomach knotting in fear. The rain, although making discovery less likely, would also make crossing more treacherous. Carlos studied me for a moment, no doubt wondering — as I was — if I was up to this, then began to work his way across the river.

The moon had not yet risen and clouds hid the stars. The darkness was like a black fog. Carlos was a vague blur ahead of me, moving agilely from rock to tree to rock. I knew better than to look down at the raging water. I followed as quickly as I dared, but there was one narrow tree trunk that terrified me. Although I could swim, I knew that falling into the river among those rocks could be fatal — as I/Juanito had discovered. Carlos, balancing like a high-wire dancer, walked gracefully across the slippery trunk. I hesitated, then, admitting my sense of balance was nowhere near that good, sat on the tree and scooted across it while Carlos watched with ill-concealed amusement.

Slowly I inched across, my hands slippery from rain and slime. Standing near the end of the tree, Carlos reached for me — but our combined weight was too much and suddenly I was being sucked into the raging current. I grabbed for Carlos hand, missed, and slammed against a rock. I gasped in pain and my head went under, filling my lungs with water. Panic seized me and I thrashed helplessly as the darkness began to close around me.

Suddenly I heard a voice in my head — not Carlos' — say calmly, "Grab the branch in front of you."

I reached out blindly and pulled myself up. Strong hands pulled me out of the water, and I collapsed on the ground, retching and trembling.

Carlos pounded me on the back until I was able to draw a huge breath of relief. Slowly I dragged myself to a sitting position, shivering. Obviously worried, Carlos wrapped a blanket around me. "Can you move?" he asked. "We must get away from the river."

"Give me a minute," I panted. Slowly I levered myself to my feet like a drunk staggering up from the gutter. Carlos put his arm around me and urged me gently toward the woods.

"I should make a fire, but it is not safe and would be very difficult in the rain," he whispered. "Perhaps if we walk you will warm up."

"Let me rest for a few minutes," I said. "I feel as if I'm made of old seaweed." I slumped against a tree and rested my head on my knees, still trembling.

Carlos squatted in front of me, concern etched in every line of his face. But I noticed he scanned our surroundings constantly, watching and listening.

Finally I pushed myself to my feet. "Let's try it," I murmured. But as soon as I stood up, my head whirled.

Carlos grabbed me and kept me upright. After a moment I said, "I think I can do it if you'll help."

Weakly I leaned on his shoulder and put one foot in front of the other. But after a few false starts I was able to walk — totter — on my own.

"Why aren't they watching the crossing?" I whispered when I was finally able to use my voice.

Carlos shrugged. "I do not believe they know about this one — yet. They have roaming patrols, which we must be careful to avoid, but they will not be very active in this rain."

Suddenly he pulled me into the underbrush and put a finger to my lips. I heard them then — voices not far from us. Soaked to the skin, trembling, we hunched down and waited. I couldn't make out any words, but I suspected it was one of the military patrols. Carlos waited a long time after they had passed, then cautiously peered around the bushes, listening carefully. Finally he motioned me to follow and we crept slowly through the woods, all senses alert, grateful that the rain muted our footsteps. An owl hooted again and I jumped. Carlos glanced back at me, then continued on. I tried to hurry to catch up.

"Carlos," I murmured, "You were only going to take me as far as the border."

He stared at me solemnly. "You do not know the way. You would never make it alone."

"Yes, but you're putting yourself in danger. I don't ask you to do that."

"My father would never be able to hold his head up among his friends if his son abandoned a woman — a friend — alone in the wilderness." He adjusted his shoulder pack and strode on.

We walked the rest of the night. Sometimes I think I must have been asleep on my feet, for I remember little of that trek. I know we crossed miles of scrubland, then more miles of heavy undergrowth. I lost all sense of direction, but Carlos obviously knew precisely where he was going, and I suspected again that he had done this many times before. Mercifully, the rain stopped after an hour or so but clouds hid the moon. Carlos marched on with cautious assurance. Shivering and bedraggled, I followed.

Sometime after dawn, we stopped to eat and rest in a small copse. By now I was grateful for the coca leaves. If they were addictive, I'd have to worry about that later, for I knew they were keeping me going. The rising sun dried our clothing and I was feeling almost human by the time we wound our way back to the road. I suggested we would be safer out of sight in the woods, but Carlos shook his head. "From here on, there will be much traffic on the road, and we will not attract as much attention as we might if a patrol found us lurking in the trees." At least it was easier to walk on the road, which at this point was quite a bit wider and better-maintained — except for the gaping potholes — than it had been where the truck picked us up. And he was right — it was chaotic with pedestrian and vehicular traffic. Although the area looked increasingly familiar to me, I said nothing to Carlos of my conviction that I'd been here before — many times.

There — yes! — just beyond the sharp bend in the road there would be a heavy growth of brambles and then the cave-like formation of fallen trees and debris where I, as Juanito, had waited for Dominique. There would be a little stream trickling from it, unless it had dried up in the summer heat. I lagged behind Carlos, afraid to look, afraid not to look. My breath came in nervous gasps, and just as we rounded the bend, I saw it. The brambles had been cut down, and the little stream was a mere trickle. Someone had obviously reinforced the cave roof, but it was the same cave.

I must have screamed, for Carlos came running back. "What is it, *señora*? Are you all right?"

I couldn't take my eyes off the cave. I could have imagined all the rest of it: the rocks where Carlos and I had hidden last night could have simply become part of my dream about Juanito. But I had never seen this place before — not in this lifetime. Aware I was trembling, I stammered, "I thought I saw something — something in the trees. I'm sorry — I guess I'm tired and my imagination is playing tricks."

For a long moment he studied me, then took my arm. "The digging place is not far. Perhaps we can rest near there. Come."

It was late afternoon by the time we reached the archaeological site at the temple ruins. As we watched the camp from the underbrush on a small hill, the idea I had been working on suddenly took shape.

"Carlos, I'm going down there."

He glanced at me sharply.

"My father was an archaeologist — one of those diggers," I hurried to explain, "and you said there are Americans there. Maybe they can help."

"Natives are not allowed in the compound."

"But I'm not a native."

He grinned. "You almost look like one."

I didn't have a mirror, but after my involuntary swim and a rainy night in the woods, I must have looked as bedraggled as any poverty-stricken peasant. I tried to comb my hair with my fingers, but I doubt I improved things much. I thought for a moment, then dug in my shoulder pack for a comb. "But I speak English," I whispered. "It's worth a try. Can you wait for me here? Or do you need to go home?"

He shook his head. "I will wait."

I touched his arm. "Carlos, I haven't told you how much I appreciate your help. I never could have done this without you." My voice caught on tears. "Thank you — more than I know how to say."

Suddenly I saw the same sorrow in his eyes I had seen in his father's. "*Señora* — Consuela," he pleaded, "please be careful. You will. . . You are. . ." He swallowed and clamped his jaw shut but tears rose in his eyes.

"I know, Carlos, I know. And it doesn't matter. Remember that."

He stared at me in surprise, but I moved out of the bush and down the hill before he could reply.

The site was crudely fenced by yellow caution tape. Signs in English, Spanish, and what I assumed was the Indian dialect warned against trespassing. I grinned. With illiteracy at something like 95%, I doubted anyone but the archaeologists could read the warnings. I slipped inside the barrier and was immediately accosted by a tall angry woman in a huge straw hat. "Go away!" she shouted in Spanish, making shooing motions with her large brown hands. "You're not allowed in here!" I swung around and drew myself up to my full 4'10".

"Who's in charge here?" I demanded in English.

She gaped at me. "Who are you?"

"I am Dr. Consuela Rodríguez from the Archaeology and Paleoenvironmental Department at the University of Florida. Who is in charge of this dig, please?"

She hesitated, eyeing my dirt-streaked face and rags dubiously. I sighed one of Trevor's theatrically gusty sighs. "I'm from the archaeological site at Tihuanaca. My jeep broke down about 20 miles south of Tarija and I walked from there. Could I please see the person in charge? It's very important."

"You walked here alone?"

"I had a guide."

She hesitated just long enough to let me know she wasn't buying it, then said, "I'll get Dr. Brandt."

"Jackson Brandt?"

"You know him?"

"He's a colleague of my father's."

She hesitated again, obviously waiting for me to explain who my father was, but when I didn't, she shrugged and turned away. "Wait here."

In a few minutes she reappeared followed by a tall thin man with a small paunch. Stooped and silver-haired, he regarded me with suspicious ice-blue eyes. "Can I help you?"

"I'm Dr. Consuela Rodríguez from the Archaeology and Paleoenvironmental department at the University of Florida," I repeated. "You knew my father, Evan Emerssen."

"The name sounds familiar."

"It's been nearly forty years since you were on a dig together in Peru. He created quite a fuss by marrying one of the local girls."

Suddenly his face was transformed by a huge smile. There was a gap between his front teeth, and irrelevantly I remembered Papá saying Brandt had a habit of whistling through it when he was scheming. "And you're their daughter?"

"Yes. Consuela was also my mother's name."

"I remember now. She was a beautiful girl. It wasn't hard to see why your father was so taken with her. You look very much like her — at least as I remember her."

I blushed. "Thank you. Uh. . . could we speak in private, Dr. Brandt?" His assistant scowled. On his guard again, Dr. Brandt hesitated and eyed my ragged clothing. "My jeep broke down about 20 miles outside Tarija and I had to walk," I explained. "It's kind of important."

Reluctantly he led the way and I tried to smile my gratitude at his assistant as we passed. His tent was cluttered with artifacts, books, and testing equipment. Moving some books off a chair, he motioned me to sit while he moved more books and papers off the camp bed.

"You've made some interesting discoveries here," I commented. "It's beginning to look as if the Clovis people really weren't the first humans to roam the Americas."

Brandt nodded. "Some of the artifacts we've recovered date about 1,000 years before the oldest Clovis sites. Our finds seem to corroborate Dillehay's work in southern Chile. We're pretty excited about it."

I was debating whether to reveal my real name when he said, "So you're an archaeologist like your father?"

"Actually, no. I'm a psychologist, working with the archaeology department at the University of Florida," I improvised quickly. "They're doing an experimental study on the political climate during the heyday of the Tihuanacan culture, and they're hoping psychology can give them some insights."

He nodded. "A bit far-fetched, but those folks at the U of F always were rather avant-garde."

"Quite frankly, I agree with you — but it gave me an excuse to come to South America."

"Searching for your roots?"

I hesitated. Trying to keep the tremor out of my voice, I replied, "No, I came searching for a friend, Dr. Brandt. A very dear friend."

He frowned but said nothing.

"I met a photojournalist about a year ago. We fell in love and were planning to be married, but he had one more assignment in Nueva Sangria. It was to be a simple two-day job, but something went wrong and he was arrested. I couldn't get any help from any of the government agencies. Apparently the United States has little or no diplomatic relations with Nueva Sangria."

"Except for their drug eradication teams," he sniped.

"I don't know much about that except that it has become a major issue here."

"You could say that." There a strange intensity in his stare.

"Anyhow, I believe he is being held here, in Río Negro, if he's still alive." My voice wavered on tears.

Brandt whistled softly through his front teeth, studying me intently. "What is this man's name?"

"Trevor West Elliot. He's. . ." Brandt's sharp intake of breath stopped me. "Have you seen him? Do you know where he is?" In my excitement I knocked over a stack of books.

"Calm down, Dr. Rodríguez. Yes, I've seen him. He's being held in the fortress in Río Negro."

"Is he all right? Are they going to let him go?"

"Easy, easy. He's all right. For now."

His assistant's voice came from outside the tent. "Dr. Brandt, may I see you for a moment, please?"

He excused himself and, unable to sit still, I paced the small tent as voices murmured outside.

When Brandt reappeared, there was a dangerous glitter in his eyes. "I think you have some explaining to do, young lady. My assistant did some checking and she tells me there is no Consuela Rodríguez on the staff of the University of Florida. Exactly who are you and what do you want?"

To my shame, tears of exhaustion and worry slid down my cheeks. "I'm sorry, Dr. Brandt. I should have told you the truth, but it has been a harrowing few weeks and I guess I'm not thinking clearly."

Brandt waited.

"I really am Evan Emerssen's daughter. My name is Daphne Consuela Morris and I own an import business in upstate New York and I really am here to try to do something about Trevor's situation."

"Why should I believe you?" His voice was icy, but there was less suspicion in his eyes.

I shrugged. "I have no proof, of course. I have a passport, but I left it with a friend — a business associate — in Tarija because I thought if I was caught with it, I might wind up in a cell next to Trevor. I've got to get him out, Dr. Brandt. He's . . . he's . . . he's very important to me."

Brandt studied me for a long time, whistling softly.

Finally he said, "What was your mother's full name?"

"Maria Consuela Evita Quiroga de la Rosa. She was a second-year archaeological student at the dig a few miles from Quillabama."

"And what did your father call her?"

"Connie. And she hated it." Suddenly I remembered something else. "And Papá called you The Fox because he thought you were so cunning."

Brandt relaxed slightly, a bemused smile on his face. "I wasn't supposed to know that, of course. But I always thought it a bit of a compliment."

"Papá had — still has — enormous respect for you." *Actually, he said you're a prig who wouldn't do anything to jeopardize your professional reputation, but you're my only hope right now.*

"What happened after they left Peru? I lost track of him."

"My brother was born exactly nine months after they were married, so suddenly Papá had a family to feed, and his little escapade in Peru didn't sit too well with the academic community. He wound up selling insurance, then became an investment broker — did quite well. He was a great help when I set up my own business."

"Where is your family now? Are your parents still alive?"

"Oh, yes. I have two sisters and a brother. My parents live in Chicago and they're both well and still very much in love. I'll write their address down for you — I know Papá would love to hear from you." That wasn't precisely true, but this didn't seem a good time to bring up old academic rivalries.

He gestured to a writing pad near me and said, "Perhaps I should contact him now."

"I'd be happy to give you his phone number and e-mail address, but I think you'd find he'd be less than enthusiastic about my being here. The last time I talked to him, he insisted I stay home and forget about Trevor.

But I can't, Dr. Brandt. . . I just can't."

A smile flitted across his eyes. "He has a lot of room to talk about crimes of passion."

"I pointed that out. He didn't like it."

Brandt chuckled. "He always did maintain something of a double standard."

The pot calling the kettle black? Aloud, I said, "You said you'd seen Trevor. Did you actually talk to him? How is he?"

Brandt nodded. "The current administration, such as it is, thinks he represents a big news conglomerate in the States, and they're hoping to ransom him. They asked me to act as go-between. We have sporadic internet and telephone contact with the States, and I agreed because I try to maintain good relations with the locals. They allowed me to see your friend when I insisted I couldn't contact anybody in the States without more information. Mostly I wanted to see the guy and find out whether he was legit."

"Is he okay?"

"He's fine — at least as 'fine' as can be expected. Mostly, my dear, he's worried about you. He asked me to contact you, but everyone I talked to said you'd disappeared, and Elliot was beside himself."

"When was the last time you saw him? How often do you get to see him?"

"I spoke to him a couple days ago. I try not to go there often because I don't want the captain in charge to get suspicious. But I already know there's not going to be any help from Milltown Oil."

"I know — I tried to contact the bastards and they claimed they've never heard of Trevor Elliot."

Brandt nodded. "I've been stringing Captain Ortiz along, muttering about diplomatic red tape and saying my contacts in the States are trying to figure out the best way to handle this. But I've given him the impression it's only a matter of time before they pay big bucks to get their star reporter back." He raised his hands and shrugged in a gesture of futility. "That isn't going to work forever."

Tears prickled my eyes again. "I've *got* to get him out."

"What do you plan to do?"

"I wish I knew. I've thought of a hundred plans, but everything I came up with has a major flaw. Can you think of anything?" I brushed hair out of my eyes and noticed my hands were filthy.

"Not at the moment. I do think, however, that you should maintain your Dr. Consuela Rodríguez persona. If your true identity and reason for being here are discovered, you could easily wind up, as you said, in a cell — or worse."

"What about your assistant?" I asked.

"Who?"

"The woman I spoke to first."

"Oh. Dr. Tyler. Yes, that could be a bit of a problem." He thought for a moment. "I think it would be best to let her know that, although you're not officially associated with the U of F, you are a scholar of some sort, maybe working on a classified project or something — some sort of consulting work — or maybe undercover work for a drug enforcement team. The people on the dig don't socialize much with the locals because there's been an outbreak of bubonic plague near here, so we should be able to keep the truth contained."

"I have no right to ask this, but since you're involved already, is there any way you could get me in to see Trevor — maybe say I'm a representative of Milltown Oil or something?"

Brandt dropped his eyes. "I don't see how I could, without endangering our work here. You must understand we're here by the grace of the Nueva Sangrian government. I don't even want to think about what would happen if one of my 'colleagues' got involved in the local politics."

And one of my family already rattled your secure little cage too much, didn't he? I remembered then that Papá had said Brandt was cunning as a fox at getting out of anything he didn't want to do. So there it was, in simple words and quiet evasions: I was on my own. Suddenly I understood why Papá didn't like Brandt much. I rose wearily, trying to hide the anger surging through me.

"I'm sorry, Daphne — Consuela — truly I am. I'll try to get a message to Elliot, but I don't see that I can do much else. I have to think of the safety of my people here at the dig."

And if a man's life is in danger, well, that's his problem, right? Tears of frustration locked my throat. "Thank you," I finally managed. "I'd appreciate that. And if. . . if I shouldn't succeed, Dr. Brandt, would you be kind enough to let my parents know I love them?"

He hesitated, then held out his hand. "Of course. Good luck."

I gave his hand a perfunctory shake and stalked out of the tent.

16

"We will stay with my cousin in Río Negro," Carlos said. He stood up, handed me my shoulder pack, and cautiously moved back toward the road. "But I am not sure that you should have talked to this man Brandt. I think he should not be trusted."

"I hope you're wrong, but I'm afraid you're probably right — but, Carlos, I can't ask you to get any more involved. It's too dangerous."

He smiled thinly. "Cousin Consuela, I am already involved."

"Yes, but. . ."

He held up his hand. "I do not know if we can get your friend out of prison, but we must try. And I must find you a place to sleep." He hesitated. "And perhaps it is best that you know something else. Remember you said I appeared to know where I was going — had made the journey many times?"

I nodded.

"I have for some time been a *contrabandista*."

I stumbled and Carlos grabbed my arm. "A smuggler? What do you smuggle?"

He shrugged. "Whatever is available. Cigarettes mostly, sometimes . . . other things. And I watch what is happening. Information is very valuable."

"Who do you sell the information to?"

"It is best you do not know that, Cousin Consuela. The government of Nueva Sangria would be very, very unhappy if it knew what I know about them."

This was an entirely different Carlos. His eyes glittered hard and cold, and he looked fifteen years older. Suddenly my whole body was bathed in chills. I had been wandering for two days in the wilderness with a smuggler — a criminal — a gangster — who could have robbed, raped and murdered me and no one would ever have found my body. Trusting, naïve, stupid *gringa*! Uneasily I recalled the men who had gathered in José's living room that night — their furtive, almost sneaky, demeanor. I had assumed they were José's or Carlos' friends — but I realized now they must be accomplices — thugs. Obtaining weapons must have been laughably easy for them.

But Carlos acted so . . . *nice* — so courteous and friendly. Was he simply leading me on, using his charm, guessing I had a lot more cash than I had admitted? Was this trek just a way to win my trust and steal my money? But he had had many opportunities already. He could have simply hit me on the head and grabbed my shoulder pack, leaving me to wander lost and terrified in the wilderness until I died of hunger or thirst or was killed by wild animals or bandits — or he could have let me drown. *"Poor dumb American tourist — out of her league — serves her right. She should've stayed home."* And was the money still in my shoulder pack? Carlos had had it while I was with Brandt. . . *How much longer will he keep me alive?*

But Carlos was my only hope now. He trusted me with this information — I must trust him with my life.

With an effort, I put my suspicions aside.

"Does your father know?"

"This is not the United States," Carlos replied. "Here smuggling and robbery are a way of life. It is the only way to survive. My family — most families — would starve without the black market trade."

"Carlos — why are you doing this?"

"I told you — it is the only way to survive."

"No, I mean why are you helping me?"

He shrugged. "You are my father's friend. You need help." But something glinted behind his eyes and I shivered again. He hadn't told me all of it, of that I was sure. Was he a member of Eye of the Tiger?

As we approached Río Negro, the traffic increased until we were forced to walk on the shoulder of the road to keep from getting run over by honking cars and trucks, donkey carts, and bicycles. Everyone appeared to be in a hurry, but nobody was moving very fast. I realized the cacophony was, to these people, as natural and important as breathing.

We entered the city by a back road, avoiding the main streets, and it became apparent the word "city" was an overstatement. Carlos said the official population of Río Negro couldn't be over 5,000, but the slums more than tripled that figure. Unpaved and rutted, the streets would become a river of mud during the rainy season — and, judging by the smell, there was no indoor plumbing. Dirty brown streams ran along both sides of the road. Most of the dwellings were made of pasteboard boxes, newspaper and ingenuity. Naked children sat listlessly in the scorching afternoon sun among chickens pecking listlessly in the dirt.

The whole place was listless, without hope or joy. A skeletal dog panting in a small patch of shade raised its head and growled when we passed, but couldn't summon the energy to bark. A woman's voice shrilled, a man snarled in reply, and somewhere a baby wailed. Dust was everywhere, coating everything — including the emaciated children. I saw signs of rickets, and one child with gaping sores on her face picked indifferently at a scab, her eyes empty.

Carlos noticed my horror. "These are the lucky ones. They have shelter. Many do not, and roam the city looking for a handout or something to steal. Please keep a firm grip on your shoulder pack and stay near me."

"They may have shelter," I replied, "but obviously they're starving. Those children need food and clothing."

"Luxuries almost impossible for these people to obtain. Most of them have no work at all, and when they can get it, it is for pennies a day. If the girl children survive long enough, they can sell them to the slavers or *cocaleros.*"

I shuddered. "But there are countries — the United States, for instance — that provide food and clothing to poverty-stricken countries. Can't they help?"

Carlos' smile was wintry. "The United States has cut off all aid to Nueva Sangria because it has not stopped growing coca. But it would make no difference anyway — when aid does come, it never reaches these people. The food sits in warehouses until it rots because the right people have not received the right bribes — taxes, they call them. The clothing and best food go to those in favor in the government. Do you see now, Consuela, why stealing and smuggling are a way of life for these people? There is no other way. Not here. A stolen carton of cigarettes, sold on the black market, could feed one of these children for a month."

Suddenly a woman screamed — a high, hysterical shriek that ripped up my spine. I whirled, but Carlos grabbed my arm roughly, pinning me to his side. "Do not interfere. This is not your country, and not your business. Just keep walking." The shriek was abruptly cut off as if her throat had been cut, and the silence was more terrifying than the screaming. I felt tears on my face, and I realized I didn't care how Carlos made his living — I was deeply grateful for his companionship. Trembling, I clung to his arm, aware of the hard, reassuring muscle through his thin shirt.

Leaving the ghetto behind, we entered a section of permanent buildings built mostly of adobe. Small dark shops displayed their few wares, and the streets had once been paved with cobblestones — but here, too, a stinking brown stream ran on each side of the road. At an open-air cantina someone plucked at a guitar and for the first time I heard laughter.

Rosalia's husband was the proprietor of a small hotel and *cantina* not far from the fortress. She greeted her cousin Carlos with delight, but seemed less enthusiastic about his companion. I smiled and extended my hand, remembering the proper Spanish greeting, but she ignored me and stared accusingly at Carlos. There was a rapid exchange in dialect; I recognized enough of the words to guess Rosalia was asking who I was and what did he think he was doing bringing his fancy woman here?

Pretending not to understand, I listened blank-faced as Carlos gave her an abbreviated version of my story. I was a Peruvian scientist, now living in the United States, and the *gringo* in the fortress was my man — I had come to try to get him out.

How did we know he was there? she wanted to know. Carlos shrugged — we had heard rumors, and it made sense. Stupid *gringos* were always being arrested and held for ransom here.

Did we expect to stay here — at her respectable inn? Carlos smiled and said something I didn't catch. She gave me a cold, appraising look and led the way through the hotel and out through the back to a small shed. "It's all I have," she snapped in Spanish to be sure I understood.

My heart sank. The place was filthy and, I suspected,

full of bugs. I looked my plea at Carlos, and I could see the embarrassment in his eyes. "Please tell her I can pay for a room," I whispered. "I don't have much, but I can't stay here."

Motioning me to stay where I was, Carlos took Rosalia by the arm and led her out of earshot. I thought I heard the phrase *El Ojo del Tigre,* but I couldn't be sure. I didn't have to understand the words to know the argument got pretty heated, and I was about to suggest we find another place, but Carlos turned on the charm and gradually won his cousin over until he had her laughing. Swatting him playfully on the arm, she walked away shaking her head. Carlos smiled at me. "Come," he said, "we will stay."

"Here?"

"*Sí.* But in a better room."

"Your cousin doesn't seem to like me."

"You must not worry too much about Rosalia. She has a sharp tongue, but she is really very kind."

I doubted that, but said nothing as Carlos led me to a room off the back garden. "It is not large, but it will do for our needs," he explained. I eyed the one narrow bed nervously. It would be adequate for two people who were comfortable sleeping together, but not for two strangers. Carlos smiled. "I will sleep on the floor." I nodded in relief, remembering that at José's everyone slept on the floor.

"The toilet is at the other end of the garden," Carlos answered my searching gaze, "and the bath. But there is only cold water until the dinner hour."

"I guess I can wait," I replied dubiously. "I'll take a bath before dinner."

He smiled. "If you don't mind waiting in line."

I hadn't thought of that — and suddenly a cold bath sounded better than none at all.

Over dinner — served by a harried young barmaid who nevertheless found time to flirt with Carlos — we tried to decide what to do next.

"It would be best," Carlos told me, "for you to become an accepted part of the village."

"How am I going to do that? I know I look like a *gringa*, no matter what I do."

He nodded. "You will do menial tasks around the cantina, and you will allow people to discover that you are originally from Peru. You studied in the States but now are running from an abusive lover, perhaps. You have come here to work for your cousin Rosalia. The more they see you busy here, the more they will accept you. But you must do your best to keep your face hidden, for by that they will know you are not one of us."

"Are you sure Rosalia will agree to this?"

Carlos nodded. "I have already spoken to her. In the meantime, I will make contact with those I trust here, ask questions, get as much information as I can. At least we know your friend is still alive, and as long as he remains in prison, we can work to get him out. I have some friends who may be able to alert me if he is to be moved or . . . or something.

"However," he added before I had time to think about what "something" meant, "it is very important that you speak to no one about this matter. If someone mentions your friend, act as if you do not know what they're talking about. You must not trust anyone except Rosalia and myself. There are many enemies in this country, and they wear many disguises. And never mention his name. He is your friend. That is enough."

Later, in our room, I said, "Carlos — I asked you this once before, but you never really answered me. Why are you helping me?"

"That does not matter."

"It does to me."

Carolos stared at me without a word, and I wondered if I'd gone too far.

When he finally spoke, his voice was barely above a

whisper. "I had a sister who was in love with one of the soldiers in the army. My father tried to make her stay away from him, but she would not listen. He was big and handsome and had a lot of money and would drive in from Río Negro in his army vehicle to see her. One evening she slipped away to meet him secretly. She told me, but made me promise not to tell Father. That night she did not come back. We waited for several days, until I finally broke down and confessed. I thought it would kill Father, and I promised him I would try to find her."

He broke off, staring at a spot on the floor — staring into the past.

"And did you find her?" I wasn't sure I wanted to hear the answer. My thoughts went to quiet, gentle José; he had never had never even hinted to me that he was suffering. And I realized I could never really fathom that kind of pain.

Finally Carlos nodded. "I had friends in the fortress — they had heard some things. There were several soldiers involved. I found her body in a shallow grave not far from the fortress. I lured the first soldier, with nude pictures of little girls, to a deserted place, then I killed him and put his body where I had seen signs of a recent wildcat kill. By the time they found him, he was unrecognizable."

His head came up, his face haggard. "It may take the rest of my life, but I will find the other soldiers, too. It won't bring her back. Nothing ever will. But there is no going back for me, either."

Early the next morning Rosalia came to our room with a bundle under her arm, and she and Carlos swiftly transformed me into one more faceless and downtrodden citizen of Río Negro. Rosalia pulled my hair — which Trevor had always loved flowing freely to my shoulders

— into a mangy bun at the back of my neck, a style I had always hated; it made me look ten years older. Carlos smeared dirt on my face and warned me to add more every time I washed. A shapeless black dress came nearly to my ankles, covered by a stained apron. Somewhere Rosalia had even found shoes almost my size, but they were already worn and split, so Carlos encouraged them to fit better with judicious slices of a razor-sharp knife. An ugly black woolen shawl completed my disguise.

"You are discouraged by life," Carlos instructed me. "You must not walk tall and straight as you normally do, but with a bent-over shuffle — so. . ." and he demonstrated. I watched in amazement as his entire demeanor changed, taking on the bored, sullen, empty expression and foot-dragging shuffle of a man who had never had any hope in his life and never would. "Rosalia will complain that you do not move fast enough, that you are lazy and incompetent, and so you must become. Ignore her and continue to shuffle through your miserable, boring day. Very soon everyone will ignore you — you will become as unnoticeable as a fly on the wall. Then you will be able to hover and listen to conversations, pick up information, and no one will even notice you are there."

Dubiously, I let my shoulders slump and shuffled slowly across the room.

"No, no," Carlos said. "You look as if you are pretending to be discouraged. You must truly *become* discouraged. You must allow yourself to lose all hope."

"You are not a rich *gringa* from the United States," Rosalia added. "You are an ugly woman nobody wants, who has lived her entire life without joy or hope. You are nothing — nobody. You are only here because your cousin Rosalia took pity on you. Your work is sloppy, your attitude is worse. There is no hope for you — there never will be."

"And yet," Carlos pointed out, "while you are becoming this embittered, unhappy woman, old before her time, you must also watch and listen — but never allow anyone to guess you are interested in anything at all. You are bored with life, you have no hope. You are nothing — less than a fly on the wall."

"But I don't understand the local dialect," I objected. "How can I listen if I don't know what they're saying?"

Rosalia answered that one: "Most of the soldiers will speak Spanish; they come from all over the continent."

"What about the people who saw me arrive with you, Carlos? I saw many of them watching us, wondering who I was. I know they knew I wasn't a native."

"People disappear overnight here all the time — no one will ask questions. You no longer exist as Consuela. You are Maria Pérez, a nobody — a nothing. If anyone asks me what happened to that other lady, I will look alarmed and say I know nothing, which will tell them all they need to know — they will imagine the rest."

It was as if a part of me were standing off, watching my death, for I as I began to *think* of myself as wretched, miserable and unhappy, I became that way. I felt as if a sooty black cloud of hopelessness surrounded me. Involuntarily, I uttered a deep, despondent sigh and slogged my way across the room. Every step was an effort. It was early morning, but already I was tired, weighed down by miseries I couldn't fathom. Listlessly I picked up a cloth and dusted a table, but the effort was almost more than I could muster and, if the table had truly been dusty, not much would have changed with my efforts. I was close to tears of despair.

Carlos' delighted laugh startled me out of my misery. "Wonderful, Maria, wonderful! You are a born actress. Now you must continue to be poor, miserable Maria."

And so the days passed. Rosalia kept an eye on me, but was careful not to overdo her nagging and so draw too much attention to her slatternly cousin. I heard her complain to some of the regular customers that I was worse than useless, and a few of them half-heartedly tried to defend me. Her husband ignored me, as he appeared to ignore every female, including Rosalia. A perfectionist and neat-freak, I had to restrain myself from becoming a whirlwind of activity, cleaning everything in sight, but soon, true to Carlos' prediction, nobody noticed me.

I cleaned — well, sort of cleaned — a table next to a couple of men who were discussing how they were going to dispose of an entire shipment of porn videos they had hijacked the day before. They never noticed I was there — and the amount of money they were discussing was impressive. *Pornography videos? In this primitive place?* A comment from one of the men answered my question: the soldiers at the *fortaleza* — fortress — enjoyed the latest technology, thanks to the black market.

There was a side effect I hadn't expected: as I drifted listlessly around the bar, wiping the occasional table and serving the occasional beer, I began to understand more and more of the local dialect, although I was careful to mumble only heavily-accented Peruvian Spanish and pretend ignorance when anyone addressed me in Queterá beyond the simplest of words. Fortunately, the Queterá words for beer and wine were similar to the Spanish.

It became something of a game for me, and I realized with satisfaction that I was good at it. But the late evenings were what I lived for, when Carlos would saunter casually past me, often feigning drunkenness and smelling of alcohol. Careful to wait until I was sure I was unobserved, I slipped into our room to hear what he had learned that day. His contacts must have been extensive, for he brought back a lot of information.

"He is in a cell in the fourth floor — the top floor — of the *fortaleza*," he told me. "That is also where Capitán Ortiz has his office. The entire floor is heavily guarded, but no one can tell me how many soldiers are actually on guard at any time, and there is no set time for a change of guard. Apparently it happens whenever they feel like it. There are three stairways to that floor and all are barricaded and guarded. We would have to reach his cell on the fourth floor without detection, figure out how to get the key to his cell door, and get him out. At every moment we risk someone sounding an alarm, and, although we may overpower guards on one stairway, other soldiers could come up the other two."

He studied me for a moment, compassion huge in his eyes. "And we must consider that he may not be able to move fast."

I gasped. "Have they tortured him?"

"Not as far as I can tell. But, knowing Ortiz, I would not be surprised." Something dark and ugly moved behind Carlos' eyes. "He may wait until he is sure there is no hope of ransom — but Ortiz likes to think of his prisoners as toys for his amusement."

My heart sank and tears stung my eyes. *Oh, Trevor my love, hold on!*

Then a thought struck me: "Carlos, was Ortiz one of . . . one of those soldiers?"

An icy black stare was his only reply.

The next day Rosalia shouted at me to get my lazy ass into the kitchen — *now*. Moving as fast as I dared, I heaved a beleaguered sigh for the benefit of the one customer, propped my broom against the wall, and plodded into the kitchen where Carlos waited for me.

"I want you to take a look at the *fortaleza*," he said.

"Why?"

He hesitated. "I think you should see how difficult our problem is."

"Are you trying to tell me you think it's impossible?"

He fidgeted uncomfortably with a soup ladle. "I haven't given up yet, but . . . I think you should see it."

I glanced at Rosalia, whose attitude toward me had

softened considerably since that first day. I couldn't say she especially liked me, but in the few moments we had had to talk, it was apparent she at least sympathized with my plans. I suspected part of it was that she was relieved that her handsome young cousin hadn't sold himself to a rich-bitch *gringa*.

She nodded now, and said softly, "I will send you on an errand. The baker's shop is not far from the *fortaleza*, and you can pick up some special cakes I've ordered for a party tomorrow."

Carefully Carlos described the route. "Take your time," he cautioned. "And be very careful to always remember you are hopeless Maria who doesn't care enough to even glance at the *fortaleza* — or anything else." Then he hurried out, anxious, I knew, not to be seen talking to me.

Rosalia handed me some money. "It's hard to get lost in this town, but if you do, put the sun behind the *fortaleza* — it's visible from almost anywhere — put your back to the *fortaleza* and walk away from it. That will bring you very near the cantina."

"Maybe it would be best if I *did* get lost," I whispered. "It might give me an opportunity to look around, as if I were looking for the way home."

She nodded. "Please be careful." Then she lifted her voice as one of the barmaids came through the door. "See if you can do this without screwing it up," she shouted. "It's very simple — you go to the bakery, you pick up the cakes, you come back. Do you think you can manage that without someone holding your hand?"

I hunched my shoulders and shuffled out.

I was quite sure I could find my way to the fortress and back. As Rosalia had said, it dominated the small town. It was hard to maintain my beleaguered persona, for inside I was dancing. At least I was doing something constructive.

The bakery was easy to find by the delicious odors

coming from it, but I deliberately turned down another street and worked my way toward the fortress, dragging my feet, my head down and my shoulders bowed, the very picture of defeat.

Two soldiers strode toward me. Icy panic clutched at my throat. I hadn't thought of that problem! What if they stopped and questioned me? It took all my determination to maintain my plodding gait. One of them swore and shoved me roughly aside. I stumbled to my knees and they laughed, but paid me no more mind. Trembling, I staggered to my feet and tried not to hurry, although I glanced back once to be sure they were still walking away. I could feel blood running from one knee, and I prayed it wouldn't get infected in this filthy place.

The street ended abruptly at the fortress. A chain-link fence topped with razor wire surrounded the grounds, but suddenly I had to know, had to try to guess where Trevor was. His nearness compelled me toward the fence and I glanced up. Top floor — *oh, Trevor, where are you? Are you all right? Are you still alive?*

Tears filled my eyes. I ducked my head and wiped my face on my apron. And then I felt him, like a warm ocean wave, engulfing me, the intensity almost squeezing the breath out of me. Unable to move, I stood entranced, his love overwhelming me. Did he feel my presence? Were we truly communicating, or was I imagining it in my loneliness for him — my need? I couldn't stop the tears now.

A hand touched my shoulder and I jumped. Soldiers! I'd stayed too long! I turned in panic and nearly knocked down an old woman, dressed very much as I was in faded black. Grey hair straggled from under her scarf, and her eyes held a deep sadness. "Your man is there?" she asked softly.

Forgetting who I was supposed to be — forgetting that I wasn't supposed to understand the dialect she spoke — I nodded, remembering just in time not to speak. I pointed mutely to my throat and shook my head, tears still flowing down my face. She put her arm around me and urged me away. "Come," she said, "you must not stay here. The soldiers will come. Come with me." I resisted, trying to mime that I had an errand, but she only nodded and gently led me to a narrow gate between two buildings. Behind it was a courtyard, neatly swept, and I realized it was the rear entrance to a church yard. The quiet garden was a welcome respite. I heard a bird sing, and a golden-eyed cat watched me furtively from a low tree branch. The old woman sat on a stone bench, pulling me down beside her, studying my face, staring into my eyes. Then she nodded.

"You seek someone very dear to you, someone who loves you deeply." She took my hand and turned it over, tracing the lines in my palm. "You will find him. Your plans will succeed." Suddenly she stared into my eyes again, her own eyes filled with pain. "But you will pay a very, very high price, my child."

Trembling, I said nothing.

She sighed and murmured, "Wait here. I will bring the padre."

As she hurried away I remembered Carlos' words: "There are many enemies in this country, and they wear many disguises. Trust no one."

Not even a priest? But how did I know the old woman was going for a priest? What if she was going for the police? Suddenly I realized that I had become too reliant on my "invisibility". This was a small town — she had gotten a good look at my face and would realize I was a stranger — a *gringa*. I had blown my cover!

Voices and footsteps from the direction of the church! I jumped up and raced through the gate and down the street, turning at the first street, then the next, veering mindlessly here, then there, hoping to lose myself in the labyrinth of streets. I knew running would attract the wrong kind of attention, and I tried to hurry without appearing to, scuttling with my head down, hoping I looked intent on some important errand.

I heard no sounds of pursuit — not that I'd recognize them in this strange place. When I finally dared to look up, I was sure I would be truly lost — but after only a glance at the shops around me, I knew precisely where I was. Chills ran across my neck and down my arms as I recognized Dominique's house — only it was some sort of clothing store now. Bright dresses hung on display in front. Across and down the street was the house where Tonio had lived — the village bully whom Dominique and Juanito had been careful to avoid. And I knew how to get to Juanito's home from here — the part of the present-day city where Rosalia's cantina was located had been an open field when I lived here, and "my" house had been very near that field.

Trembling and still slightly disoriented, I did my best to fade into the shadows as I tried to figure out the best route back to the cantina. I was halfway there when I realized I had forgotten to pick up the cakes for Rosalia. I retraced my steps, picked up the cakes just as the shop was closing, and hurried back to the cantina. On the way, I passed the place where I had lived as Juanito, but it was now a weed-choked lot, and I tried not to stare.

By the time I got back to the cantina, Rosalia, obviously nearly hysterical with worry, masked it with a sharp scolding. "Where the hell have you been? The bakery is only a few streets away — did you go by way of Mexico?" I mumbled apologies and fled to the kitchen where she found me a few moments later. "Go to your room quickly without being seen," she whispered urgently, then launched into a shriek that could be heard clear to the fortress. "You damned lazy slut! Get out of my sight!"

Trying to rush without being observed, I breathed a sigh of relief as I slipped into the room I shared with Carlos. He was sitting on the bed, his face a sickly grey.

"*Madre de Dios,* you had us worried. What happened?"

Leaving out the fact that I had lived in this village before, I told him about the old woman, the church, and my flight. "I'm sorry, Carlos — I really screwed up. I was so close to him — I guess I sort of . . . well . . . lost my mind."

I broke off because he was staring at me open-mouthed.

"What's wrong?" I asked.

"You're speaking Queterá."

Oh, shit. "Uh, well . . . I've always learned languages easily. I guess I just picked it up."

It was apparent he wasn't convinced, but he changed the subject. "The old woman — did she get a good look at your face?"

I nodded sheepishly. "I guess I'm not very good at this."

He sighed. "Perhaps Rosalia knows her — can you describe her more accurately?"

I shook my head. "Just an old woman, dressed all in black, like most of the old women I've seen. Oh — she had a mole on her right — no, left — cheek. She told me our plans would succeed."

"You *told* her what you're planning?"

"No! She must have been a seer or something; she seemed to know what I was thinking, and she read my palm."

"And she had a key to the courtyard?"

"I don't think it was locked."

"What did you say to her?"

"Nothing. I remembered I wasn't supposed to speak Queterá and so I pretended I was mute." Then I realized my mistake — another one.

Carlos' voice was dangerously soft. "You do speak Queterá, then. Where did you learn it?" I could see the suspicion in his eyes and I scrambled to find a plausible explanation.

"Carlos, I swear to you I didn't understand it when I first came here. But on the truck I began to notice I was picking up a phrase here and there, and while I've been working at the cantina, listening to it all day long, I guess I learned more than I realized."

"Why should I believe you?" His voice was as cold as his eyes. "As a matter of fact, why should I believe your story about this afternoon? Where did you go today?"

"I went to the fortress as you asked me to. There I met this old woman who took me to the church, but I remembered your telling me not to trust anyone, so I ran away from her, and of course I got lost. I got halfway back here and remembered the cakes for Rosalia and had to go back to the baker's to get them. Then I came straight back here."

"What did the padre look like? What did you say to him?"

"I didn't speak to him! I told you I pretended I couldn't talk! And I never saw him. I heard him — or someone — coming toward me from the church, and that's when I ran."

"Who did you talk to inside the fortress?"

"I told you! I didn't go inside! I stood outside the fence and tried to guess where Trevor was being kept, and I missed him so much I burst into tears, which attracted the old woman, I guess. She's the only person I spoke to except the baker. Please believe me, Carlos — I swear I'm telling you the truth."

"You said you didn't speak to the woman."

"I didn't speak to her — I made gestures. *She* spoke to *me*."

"You say you got lost. Who did you ask for directions?"

"Nobody. Rosalia told me if I headed in a certain direction from the fortress, I'd get back here, and I walked until I could see the fortress and get myself oriented. That's one reason I was gone so long."

Carlos sat silent for a long time, deep in thought, while I fought the need to babble and beg. I even considered kneeling and pleading. I needed his help and trust — how much of that trust had I destroyed with my stupidity? What would keep him from turning me over to Ortiz and his soldiers or quietly disposing of my body in a ravine somewhere? Yet I feared that if I told him about remembering my past lives, he would be absolutely convinced I was either a nut case or a liar — or both.

Finally he looked at me, but there was no warmth in his eyes. "For my father's sake I will continue to help you, but I do not trust you. Remember I will always be on guard, and if the slightest harm comes to me or my father or my cousin, I will kill you. Do you understand?"

I nodded shakily. "Thank you. I understand your suspicion, but all I can do is assure you that what I've told you is the truth."

"Except that you speak Queterá like a native, and you were gone several hours this afternoon."

"The only explanation I have is the one I've given you."

"No, there is more," he said softly, his eyes killer-cold. "I don't know what it is, but there is more to your story than you have told me. I have seen you catch yourself, as if you were about to say something. You are hiding something, Consuela, or whoever you are. And I will find out what it is before this is over. You had better pray I don't dislike what I learn."

17

Having Carlos sleeping on a pallet in my room had been reassuring before. Now I tossed and turned, starting at the slightest noise, terrified he would slit my throat in the darkness. Afraid to move, afraid to breathe, I spent most of the night trying to think of some way to prove to him I was not the enemy. The small window of our room was beginning to turn grey when I finally managed to doze off.

  ∿ ∾

I swung my scythe listlessly in the heat and glanced toward the fortress behind me, where Estrellita should appear at any moment. I couldn't hide a smile as I thought of her. She had grown into a beautiful woman, and I was sick with love for her. Our families still refused to let us marry, but I was working on a plan. In a few months I would have saved enough money for us to run away. Desperately I hoped it was enough — I had so little knowledge of what was required in the outside world. But Dominique, a soldier now, assured me I was very close. "You won't have a lot to spare," he warned me, "but it should get you and Estrellita to La Paz, where you should be able to get a job." He shrugged and grinned ruefully. "With your stubbornness and charm, I expect you to be the president of the country by next year."

I glanced toward the fortress again. Where was Estrellita? She had promised to come! Then I heard a low whistle from the shadows in the woods on the opposite side of the field. Estrellita's blouse was a white blur and her face a darker blur above it. I saw her wave, but couldn't tell whether she was warning me away or beckoning me to come. Cautiously I put down my scythe and moved toward her. She disappeared into the woods, and I began to run. As I passed the first trees, Estrellita was nowhere to be seen. I stopped and stared around, and suddenly she wrapped her arms around me.

"Come, my foolish boy!" And she led me at a run through the trees to an old stone hut. She slipped through the doorway and I was right behind her. With a giggle she turned to me and pressed herself against me, her breasts soft yet firm against my chest.

I wrapped my arms around her and held tight, willing my breath to slow. My hands moved up her back, delighting in the feel of her smooth skin beneath the thin blouse. "Estrellita!" My voice was ragged. We didn't speak after that for a long, long time, the only sound our breathing and her faint happy whimpers. Finally she pushed me away.

"No more, my beloved Juanito! Not now! I want to show you something!" She took my hand and led me toward the back of the small hut, dragged an ancient tarp aside, and pulled on the handle of a trap door. Rusted hinges screeched; worn stone steps led down into absolute darkness.

"What is it?" I whispered.

*"I'm not sure. I found it yesterday when I was col-
lecting wood for the kitchens. Look, there's even a supply of candles."* She picked one up and, with a match
she had obviously stolen from the kitchen, lit the wick,
which sputtered reluctantly before it finally caught.

"Where does it go?" I whispered.

*"There's an old door behind the altar in the fortress
chapel. I'm not sure, but I think this goes to it. Let's find
out!"*

Estrellita knew me well — I couldn't resist the challenge. Taking the candle from her, I said, *"Light another one and follow me."*

The two candles didn't provide much light, but it
was enough to see that the tunnel did go in the direction of the fortress. We picked our way carefully. The
stone steps were in surprisingly good condition, and
the floor was mostly clear of debris, although seepage
and dampness stained the walls and water puddled on
the floor. I ducked just in time to avoid a huge spider
web, its deadly eight-legged guardian crouched in the
center. Estrellita let out a little scream, quickly hushed,
and we hurried on.

As we neared the fortress — I assumed we were still
headed in that direction, although we were both disoriented — we heard water dripping. The tunnel made
an abrupt turn to the left, and suddenly we found ourselves looking at a moldy old well. Water dripped from
the ceiling into the well, and there was some sort of aq-
ueduct which had apparently once fed the well.

I wrinkled my nose. *"I don't think I want to drink
that water."*

"Why would they have a well here?" she asked. Although we were whispering, our voices echoed.

*"I would guess, when the fortress was first built, this
was used to supply the place with water if they were be-
sieged."* I leaned over the edge of the well and raised my
candle, but the weak light was lost in the depths.

Estrellita clung to me and I put my arm protectively around her. "Nothing can hurt you while I'm with you," I assured her, wishing I were as certain as I hoped I sounded. A rat scuttled across my foot and I jumped. Estrellita shrieked in terror and I clamped my hand over her mouth and put my lips on her ear. "You must be silent now!" I whispered. "I think we're very near the fortress, and if they find us, you know what might happen."

Trembling, she nodded. We were both employed at the fortress — she as a kitchen maid, I as a grounds- keeper — but the areas we were allowed in were care- fully defined and those who crossed the invisible lines were severely punished. Dominique had hinted at strange goings-on in the fortress late at night, but I had always suspected he was making up the stories to scare me. Still, I wasn't sure.

Was that a moan I heard? Or a door opening? How far underground were we now? I had no way of know- ing. I pushed Estrellita behind me and moved cautious- ly toward an archway in the wall. Then I heard it again — a moan! Was it human? Trembling, I peered around the corner. Barred cells lined both sides of the tunnel. They appeared to be empty, but in one a man lay curled on a bench, moaning softly. We must have been fair- ly close to the surface, because a tiny barred window near the ceiling permitted a weak smear of grey light. I could see that his clothing was in shreds. I couldn't tell how old he was or how tall he was, but I could hear him muttering in a broken, tear-wracked voice.

I put my mouth next to Estrellita's ear and breathed, "You stay here. I'm going to find out who that is."

Eyes huge with terror, face so white it almost glowed, Estrellita grabbed my arm and tried to stop me, but I put my finger lightly on her lips and gently shoved her toward the well. "Start back," I whispered. "I'll follow in a moment." But she shook her head vio-

lently and stayed where she was.

Moving as quietly as I could, I approached the cell, then moved on past it to investigate the corridor beyond. There seemed to be no one on guard, so I returned to the cell. "Señor, can you hear me?" My voice was a croak. The man stopped whimpering and appeared to be listening, but didn't move. "Señor, this way. Can you move?"

He sat up slowly, painfully. His shirt was nothing but blood-streaked rags, his breeches in little better shape, his feet bare. Without a word, he stared at me, shielding his eyes against the candle's light. I moved forward slowly, cautiously. Like a frightened animal, he backed toward the far wall of the cell, whimpering. His skin stretched tight over his bones and his hair was grey — yet I had the impression he was much younger than he looked.

"I'm not going to hurt you," I said softly. "Who are you?"

He said nothing, and I wondered if he was deaf. Finally I reached the bars of the cell and peered through them. The prisoner looked vaguely familiar, but I couldn't place him.

"How often do the guards come down here?" I asked.

Silence. It occurred to me that he might think I was a ghost or a figment of his imagination. I drew a piece of bread, left over from lunch, out of my pocket. "Here, eat this. It's not much, but I'll bring you more." I held it toward him, but he made no move to take it. Irritably, I tossed the piece of bread toward him. Couldn't he see I was trying to help?

"Why are you here?" I asked.

Nothing.

"I'll be back as soon as I can." Then I turned and hurried toward the well where Estrellita, wide-eyed and trembling, stood where she could watch me and the prisoner.

"We've got to hurry," I whispered to her. "I have no idea when guards will come, but that man needs food and a way to get out of here."

"Juanito, you can't help him!" she whispered urgently. "All you'll do is get yourself in trouble, and maybe wind up in a cell down here too. Please, leave it alone! Forget you saw him!" Motioning her to silence, I led her quickly back to down the tunnel to the stone hut, where we closed the door and replaced the old tarp, scattering dirt and leaves on top of it, hoping it wouldn't appear disturbed. Then I pulled her outside into the sunshine.

Estrellita was white and shivering, tears running down her face. I took her tenderly into my arms and smoothed her hair. "It's all right, Estrellita. Hush, now."

"Wh . . . who w . . . was he?"

"I don't know. But I have to get him out of there."

"Juanito, no! Let it be, please!"

"I can't. You know that. I have to find some way to help."

"He's probably a thief or a murderer! He'll kill you or turn you over to the soldiers!"

"I don't think so. I have to try. Please understand."

"I'm sorry I showed you that tunnel!" She pulled away from me and ran through the trees and back across the field, disappearing through the kitchen door of the fortress. My heart heavy, I waited for a long time so no one would guess we had been together, then moved through the trees and sauntered as casually as I could into the field from another direction, where I picked up my scythe and began to mow, my mind busy.

I came awake with a gasp, the old feeling of disorientation making the room at the inn seem like another dream. Gradually I came completely awake, to find Carlos eyeing me suspiciously from his pallet, a knife ready in his hand. "I had a bad dream, Carlos. I'm so fright-ened."

18

On Monday the cantina was closed and Rosalia said I could take the day off. I simply had to get out, to walk off my fear — and find out if that secret passageway was still there. Because Carlos and Rosalia no longer trusted me, I no longer trusted them, and I began to realize I might have to do this on my own. I must begin making plans.

Plodding head-down, maintaining my downtrodden persona, I headed for the fortress and what I hoped was still an open field behind it. I tried not to think of Trevor, but all I could see in my mind was his torture-scarred body, like the body of that man in the cell. Was Trevor even alive? I took a deep breath to stop the pain in my heart. It was siesta, and the streets were deserted. I could see why — the heat was overwhelming, especially dressed as I was. The skirt may have been ragged, but it was long and heavy. In minutes I was light-headed and soaked with perspiration. I scratched a place on my head; my scalp had been itching a lot lately. Probably the soap I'd been using instead of shampoo. And

I hadn't been able to bathe nearly as often as I wanted.

As I approached the fortress, my heart sank. The wire fence around the compound included the field behind, turning south about half a mile from where I stood. Cicadas buzzed and little dust devils danced in the heat. The fortress looked deserted — siesta. I stared longingly through the wire, unable to see what was beyond, trying to remember how far the old shed had been from the fortress. Would it be outside the compound fence? *Oh, Trevor, please stay alive!*

I glanced around. An old man dozed in a doorway, but otherwise there was no one on the street. Too impatient to maintain my downtrodden shamble, I moved quickly, stopping occasionally to look behind me. But I was sure no one had seen me leave the cantina, and I doubted there would be many about in this heat. Worrying that I would be too noticeable if I stayed close to the fence, I spent most of an hour scurrying up and down side streets and dead ends. Several times I had to backtrack to get around debris or undergrowth.

At the corner of the fence, I lurched to a stop. The woods where Juanito and Estrellita had had their tryst was now a jumble of paper shacks surrounding what looked like a dump. A few feet from me, an emaciated dog snarled, careful to stay out of reach. Rabid? But rabid animals attack without warning — or do they? I had brought no weapon — not even a knife. Cursing my lack of knowledge and foresight, I hesitated, sweat and tears of frustration stinging my eyes. This was too much for me to handle alone. I thought about going back to get Carlos, but what could I say? That I'd seen this place in a dream? The secret entrance probably wasn't even there, after all these years — and if it was, I had no idea how far from the fortress it was, or where it led. The search could take days — days I didn't have.

I knew siesta would soon be over — and I wasn't sure I'd have the opportunity or courage to do this again. I moved slowly into a narrow street, trying to maintain my miserable Maria persona while studying every inch of my surroundings. Someone snored heavily, a cat yowled, a baby cried. But the overall silence was deafening. I nearly tripped over a dead rat; a cloud of flies rose from it and settled back; a few landed on my face and I waved them away in disgust. I could tell by the stench the thing had been dead a long time.

I hurried on, glancing at the fortress, worrying that I was too visible this close to the fence. But I thought I recognized the rear door Estrellita had disappeared through that afternoon long ago. The secret entrance had been — I thought — at an angle out from the other corner of the fortress — another quarter mile or so as the crow flies, but another hour or two by foot — if I was lucky. Oh, how I wished I'd asked Carlos for help!

The sun had dipped noticeably but the air was only marginally cooler. As I crept deeper into the slum, I realized siesta was over. People moved about and a dog barked — one short yelp. A woman called someone's name. Nearby a man coughed, hawked and spit. I didn't dare turn, but he sounded very close. Two cats yowled — I jumped, my heart pounding so hard I could scarcely breathe.

I was almost to the dump now, wondering which route would take me around it fastest, when a man lurched out of a doorway; from the smell, I guessed it was the local pub. His shirt was open and his feet were bare, his pants sagging below a huge hairy belly. He belched loudly and eyed me as I dipped my head in what I hoped was an I-belong-here-too gesture and moved past him — but he stepped in front of me and said something I couldn't understand. If it was Queterá, it was a different dialect from the one I knew. Either that or he was drunk. I tried to go around him, but he barred my way and repeated his challenge. I glanced up timidly and muttered something in Queterá about needing to get home to my husband. His small eyes were bloodshot and full of animal malice.

I thought he was going to let me pass, but suddenly he grabbed my arm and dragged me between two hovels. I struggled and tried to scream, but one powerful hand clamped over my mouth as he pulled me deeper into the alley. Dirt was caked on his arm. I wondered if I'd catch something from the filth on his hand, but I bit it anyway and he yelped and let go long enough to slap me across the face. I retched from the taste and my head rang from the blow. He clamped his hand over my mouth again and dragged me on. Suddenly everything went dark and I thought I'd gone blind — but as my eyes became accustomed to the gloom, I saw we were in a small storage hut. With one arm he dragged me toward a pile of rags and trash and fumbled with his trousers with the other. I drew a breath to scream, but he slammed me face-down into the filthy rags. Hands pulled at my skirt; I managed to turn over and scream, but he hit me again and the world reeled and receded. I opened my eyes to see that he had gotten his pants down and was kneeling over me, fumbling at my skirt. I kicked at him and clawed at his eyes, but he jerked his head out of the way and slapped me casually, as if slapping a mosquito. Roughly he forced my legs apart, and I tried to roll away when he fell heavily on top of me.

Screaming, I tried to push him off, but he was much too heavy — and very still. Something warm and wet trickled down my neck.

A shadow occulted the sunlight from the doorway, then moved, and my attacker was dragged off me. I squinted; all I could see was a silhouette. Momentarily dazed, I lay there, wondering if I had the strength to fight off this intruder, too. The silhouette spoke: "Get up, Consuela."

Carlos!

Sobbing with relief, I struggled to my feet. "Oh, god,

I'm glad to see you," I babbled. "Thank god you got here in time! How did you find me. I was so scared — oh, Carlos, thank you. . ."

"Shut up!" His voice, low and controlled, was scarier than a shout. I realized I'd been babbling in English. His eyes were like two black stones; his hand held a bloody knife. I glanced down at my attacker; his throat was slit from ear to ear. Without a word Carlos wiped his knife on the man's shirt, then grabbed my arm and dragged me out of the hut and down the street. I had to run to keep up with his long strides. I stumbled and he pulled me roughly to my feet. People stared and gave us a wide berth.

Outside the slum, Carlos cleaned his knife again in the dirt, sheathed it, and snapped, "Wipe the blood off your face and keep your head down." Then he set off for the cantina. I had to race to keep up, and I could feel my cheek swelling from the other man's blows.

Abruptly Carlos stopped, looking around carefully, studying every doorway. "We will walk slowly now. We are out for a stroll after siesta."

I nodded, but a thousand questions buzzed in my head. "Carlos, how did you find me? Were you following me?"

"Shut up! I am far too close to slitting your throat, too."

Trembling, I tried to emulate his casual saunter back to the cantina.

Back in our room, he faced me, his back to the locked door, his eyes pools of black fire. "Now. You will tell me all of it — everything. You will not leave out one word, or tell one lie. If you do, your body will never be found." He moved closer, towering over me, staring down into my eyes. I shivered and tried to back away, but he caught my arm roughly and twisted my elbow. "Do you understand, *señora*?"

I yelped and nodded, backing away until I dropped

onto the bed. Carlos stood in the middle of the room, legs wide, arms crossed, one hand on his knife, watching me.

My whole body was shaking. *Post-traumatic shock. Pull yourself together or he'll never believe you!* I clenched my hands in my lap and took a deep shuddering breath. "This is going to sound crazy, which is why I didn't tell you before. I didn't think you'd believe me — I still don't. But I swear to you it's the truth." Carlos stood rock still, watching. Waiting.

And so I stammered through all of it. From my weird "dreams" to my recognizing certain local landmarks — to my attempt to find the hidden underground passage. He listened without interruption, without changing expression. "I didn't tell you all of it because I thought you'd think I was crazy or lying." I sighed. "As it is, you don't trust me anyway. I was hoping I could find that secret passageway. . ." I trailed off, choking on sudden hysterical laughter.

"Then what would you have done?"

"I don't know, Carlos. I didn't think past that. M-m-maybe I hoped you'd b-b-believe me — maybe I thought I could do it myself. I j-j-just don't know."

He was silent for a moment, watching me. "My father said you had the gift," he finally replied. "I am not sure I believe all you've told me, but I think he was right that you have some sort of special sight."

I scratched at my scalp and my fingers came away bloody. I pulled a speck of black dirt out of my hair — but the speck jumped off my finger.

"Fleas! I have fleas!" I shrieked, pulling at my clothes and hair. "Get them off me!" Carlos tackled me and pinned me down on the bed with his body, one hand over my mouth. "Shut your mouth, you goddamn fool! You'll have the whole cantina in here!"

His attack somehow flipped a switch in me. I could feel something move behind my eyes, and I saw it mirrored in his. The Woman of Ice and Snow was back. Suddenly I was icily calm.

"I'm sorry," I said quietly. "I'll be fine now, I promise you."

Carlos rolled off me and stared. "What the hell are you?"

19

It was still dark when Carlos shook me awake, one hand over my mouth. "Make no sound," he whispered. "I must be gone for the day. *Do not leave the cantina!* Do you understand me?"

"Do I have the right to ask where you're going?"

"We must make our move tomorrow or not at all. I have a plan, but I need to make arrangements. I will be back about nightfall. If you leave the cantina alone again, you will have no hope or help from me or Rosalia. Do you understand me?"

I nodded. "Will you tell me what your plan is?"

"When I return. Until then, *try* to follow my orders for a change."

I'd had a lot of long and scary days lately, but this one was the worst. Rosalia alternated between ignoring me and shouting at me, but I could see she was worried, too. All day my mind raced: was Trevor in danger? Carlos' sudden urgency seemed to indicate that. But why hadn't he told me last night? Where had he gone? Was he really going to help me get Trevor out, or was he plotting my death? The delay and frustration were making all of us irritable and a little crazy. I caught myself sweeping the floor with un-Maria-like vigor. Rosalia's husband glared sullenly, accusingly, from the bar.

During siesta, unable to sleep, I paced our small room, trying to think clearly, weighing every possibility I could think of. What if Carlos had been arrested or waylaid? What if he wasn't coming back? Had he abandoned me here? No, of course not: he wouldn't leave Rosalia stuck with me. Then a sudden thought filled me with cold horror: had he insisted I stay at the cantina so I wouldn't hear what he already knew — that Trevor was dead?

By the time Carlos finally slipped through the door late that evening, I'd worked myself up to a roaring headache and a stomach full of acid.

In our room, he dropped his shoulder pack and stared at me, his eyes still cold. Impatiently I asked, "Did you get what you needed?"

He nodded. "Tomorrow afternoon *Capitán* Ortiz leaves for Tarija for the weekend. He visits a lady there regularly. He usually does not come back until Sunday afternoon, but we must not take any chances. If he is waiting for word from the United States, he may cut his stay in Tarija short."

He looked at me carefully. "Can I trust you to get to the digging place and back without getting into any more trouble?"

I returned his gaze steadily. "Yes."

"Any more foolish side trips like the last may endanger your friend. Already I have heard rumors that he may be shot. *We have no time for your stupidity! Do you understand that?*"

I nodded, forcing aside the fear that welled up: could we have come so far, only to lose Trevor now? "I understand. I assume you want me to take a message to Dr. Brandt?"

"Tell him to get a message to your friend: do *not* eat any food tomorrow after the noon meal."

"Are you sure about this? He's probably already weak. Going without food might . . ."

Carlos glared. "If he wants to get out of this alive, he must do as he is told, as you must. I can think of no other way."

"Do I get to know what you're planning?" I snapped.

"I have a friend in the kitchen at the fortress." Carlos dropped a large bag of white powder on the table. "This will be added to the evening meal. It will make the soldiers sick and they will pass out. We must do it when the *capitán* is away, because he does not eat the food prepared in the kitchen. However, my friend in the kitchen must be paid for his trouble."

I nodded. I'd long since checked my money stash, and it was still there. "How much do you need?"

"Twenty US dollars."

I dug in my shoulder bag. "Here. Give him forty."

"No. If I overpay him this time, he will expect that the next time I need a favor." He folded both bills in his pocket. "But the rest will cover the cost of the powder and my trouble. Now — you must leave immediately for the digging place. It is still early. Can you get there alone, without being noticed?"

"I think so."

"Hurry. But don't forget you are Maria, not Consuela. And come straight back." Suddenly he grabbed my arm and twisted it. "Do not forget what I said last night," he hissed.

I pulled away, picked up my shoulder bag and slipped out, aware of a sudden exhilaration: action at last! The waiting was over.

The Woman of Ice and Snow moved carefully through the streets, outwardly depressed Maria, inwardly the alert warrior, taking note of everything, moving with carefully-hidden assurance. The gods were finally smiling on me, for I met no one. The town looked deserted, and there was no traffic on the road. Vehicles were parked along the side of the road, their occupants sound asleep. It felt as if I were the last human alive.

About a mile out of town, the road became little more than a dirt track, and, in spite of the heat, I took a chance and broke into a jog. I arrived at the dig breathless, my clothes soaked with perspiration. No one stopped me, so I hurried to Dr. Brandt's tent.

"Dr. Brandt?" I called softly. "Are you there?" No response. I tried again, a little more loudly.

I was about to peek around the tent flap when Brandt appeared from the direction of the dig. "Locals are not allowed in here!" he snapped. "Go away!"

"Dr. Brandt, it's Consuela Rodríguez — Daphne Morris."

He stared for a moment, and then the name registered. "Oh — you. What do you want?"

"I need you to get a message to Trevor," I said softly, wondering if Dr. Tyler was eavesdropping around the corner.

"What sort of message?"

"Please keep your voice down. This is urgent. You must get it to him today. Tell him not to eat any food after the noon meal tomorrow."

"Why?"

"Please — just tell him I said that." I fidgeted impatiently.

"He doesn't know you're here. I haven't seen him since the last time I saw you."

"Are they preventing your visits?"

He shook his head. "I don't want to get involved. Your presence here endangers the whole operation."

"Dr. Brandt, a man's life is in danger. There are rumors that Ortiz is going to have him shot. We *have* to get him out of that fortress immediately."

"What's that got to do with the food?"

I sighed. "Since you're so concerned about your work here, don't you think you'd be better off not knowing? Just give him the message — please."

Brandt stared at me a long time. "I think you'd better leave."

"Promise me you'll take the message."

"I have a lot of work to do here, if you'll excuse me. . ."

"My father was right," I snapped. "He said you're a coward, and he was absolutely right. You won't even save a man's life if it threatens your precious dig."

"I think I've heard enough."

"No, Dr. Brandt, you haven't. Because my father has maintained his academic contacts, and, believe me, he will hear about this when I get back to the States. I ask a small favor — simply deliver a message. I don't ask you to put yourself in harm's way, but by god, you've just done so in your professional life. I'm sure Simon Harrison would love to hear how eager you were to help a compatriot in danger." It was a long shot, but I could see it had hit home: Harrison was a big name in Latin American archaeology, something I'd learned from Jim Garcia's printouts. I turned away, fighting the urge to bury my knife in Brandt's paunch.

"Wait . . ." Brandt shuffled his feet, fidgeting with his pipe. "I have to go into town to get some supplies today after siesta — I'll tell Ortiz I have some news for him, but have to talk to Elliot first."

"And what news will you have for Ortiz?"

He whistled softly through his teeth and stared at his feet. "That it's almost certain that Milltown Oil will agree to pay $100,000 for Elliot. It's not official yet, but it should be by the end of next week." He sighed. "God alone knows what will happen to us when he loses his prize bargaining chip. If we get thrown out of here — or worse — it'll be on your head!"

"Thank you," I replied softly. "That's all I ask."

By the time I got back to the outskirts of the town, I

was once again — at least outwardly — poor downtrodden Maria.

20

The night was a restless one. Kept awake scratching the flea bites which I had decided I would simply have to put up with until I got back to civilization, I'd also developed a fever — and there was a funny painful swelling inside one thigh. It was dark, like a bruise; I assumed I had pulled a muscle when I was jogging, and the fever was no doubt from exhaustion and excitement. I comforted myself with the thought that in 24 hours, it would all be over. *Hold on, Trevor my love, my life! I'm on my way!*

I'd told Carlos about my conversation with Brandt, and he shook his head. "I do not trust that one to keep his promises."

"I'm hoping I scared him enough. His precious reputation is very important to him."

But now, in the dark of the night, doubts plagued me like the fleas. What if Brandt had no intention of passing my message on? What if he had not been allowed to see Trevor? What if. . . what if. . .?

Finally, I slept.

❧   ❧

It was still dark when I crept to the stone hut and carefully opened the heavy door. I'd brought several extra candles, along with some food, water and boots I hoped would fit the prisoner. I had not told Estrellita what I was going to do; much as I loved her, I didn't trust her to keep quiet.

The tunnel seemed longer and damper and scarier than it had the last time, and eerie moanings and whisperings echoed in the passageway. The dim candlelight made weird shadows on the walls; faces seemed to leer out of the dark corners. I hurried on, moving so fast the candle went out and I had to fumble in total darkness to light it again. Trembling, I shielded it with my hand, trying to walk more carefully, narrowly missing the huge spider web again.

I heard water dripping and the well materialized out of the gloom. I passed it cautiously, my ears tuned for any unusual sound. A rat slithered into a dark corner. I thought I heard snoring and hoped it was the prisoner, not a guard dozing outside the cell. Carefully I peered around the corner, trying to allow as little light as possible down the corridor. I couldn't see if the prisoner was in his cell, but the door was closed — he was probably asleep in a corner. As far as I could see, the corridor was empty.

Slowly I moved past the cell, searching for a key, hoping it was kept on a hook somewhere nearby and not on somebody's belt. Success! A ring of keys lay on a table around the corner. But would one fit the cell door? Careful to be sure they didn't clink together, I picked them up and rushed back to the cell.

I raised my candle. He was curled on a cot, so unmoving I wondered if he was alive. "Señor," I whispered as loudly as I dared. "Are you awake?"

No answer. What if he was dead?

Quietly I tried the first key. Nothing. I'd gone through six keys, my heart pounding harder with each failure, when finally one opened the lock with a screech. The noise woke the prisoner, who covered his eyes and cowered. Carefully I slowed my breathing enough to listen for someone coming to investigate. All I heard was water dripping and that weird moaning sound which seemed to come from everywhere and was getting louder. I tried not to think of ghosts.

"Don't be afraid," I finally whispered through a dry mouth. "But we must hurry. Can you wear these?" I handed him the boots, but he simply stared wildly at me. He tried to say something, but all he could manage was something that sounded like "Ah-ee-o?"

Just then the candle burned down to my fingers and went out. I dropped the stub, sucking on a burned thumb. Swearing softly, I fumbled to light another one. Finally I got it lit to find the prisoner still staring at me, the boots in his hands.

"Put them on," I snapped. "We don't have much time."

Again he made that strange noise, then pointed to his open mouth. I moved the candle closer and I saw an ugly red stump where his tongue should have been. I turned away, retching. Suddenly I realized who the old man was: he had owned a shop near my home several years back, and had taught me my letters and sums. I couldn't remember his name, but he had been a patient teacher and I had him to thank for my promising position at the fortress — which I was now jeopardizing. If they caught us, we'd both be dead. Or worse.

"Why are you here?" I asked him.

But he only shook his head and pointed to his mouth.

"Put the boots on and let's get out of here. We'll find some way to communicate later."

It was apparent the boots were painful for him, but I didn't want to take a chance on his stepping on a rock or poisonous insect. Trying to ignore the increasing moanings and creakings from the walls, I handed the old man some bread and cheese and a bottle of water and hurried him down the dank passageway. Going was slow — he was weak — but he shuffled after me as quickly as he could, gnawing on the cheese, trying to hide his grimaces of pain. I used three candles on the return trip. The last one guttered out just before we reached the stairway, and I had to fumble in the dark to find the first step.

We stumbled up together, both of us panting with exertion now.

I'd taken a chance and left the door to the passageway open, so we moved out cautiously. The sunrise was already beginning to turn the sky grey.

"We have to find some place to hide you until dark," I whispered. "I know a small cave — it's not very comfortable, but you can stay there until I come to get you tonight." Obviously exhausted, he merely nodded.

Suddenly the trees began to make a strange creaking noise, as if in a high wind — but there was no wind. Then the earth began to heave and shake. I pulled the old man out of the hut just before it fell into a heap, and watched in horror as the tunnel we'd just left collapsed. But we were safe.

Then I heard a roaring, ripping sound behind us. Something heavy slammed against my head — and suddenly I was above the trees, looking down in astonishment at a pile of old rags under a fallen tree. It took me a moment to realize the rags were the bodies of two men — and I that I was rising like an eagle above the tops of the trees, the old man rising beside me. But he was much younger now, and completely healed. He wore a soft white tunic with billowing sleeves and low-cut boots with trousers that flared slightly at the bottom. His hair was long and dark, curling slightly at the ends, caught neatly at the nape of his neck with a silver clasp. "We almost made it, Juanito," he laughed. "My thanks." And then he disappeared.

❧　❧

I lay awake in the dark hour before dawn and thought about what I'd seen, grumbling to myself that if I'd had that dream earlier, it would have saved both Carlos and me a lot of trouble, wishing I could ask LuAnne if these dreams were prophetic. Why hadn't I realized before that the old man was Trevor? And did this mean neither Trevor nor I would survive? I couldn't accept that — I must keep believing I would get him out. At least I knew there was no hope of using that secret passageway.

I must have dozed again, because when Carlos woke me later, I felt as if that tree were still on top of me. Groggy and feverish, I wanted nothing more than to roll over and go back to sleep. "Wake up!" he snapped. "We have work to do."

Preparations, plans, discussions — Carlos insisted on going over everything in minute detail. I couldn't see the point; we had no real idea what we were facing. Somehow I muddled through the day, my head heavy and full of dust and mist. In spite of the heat, I was so cold my bones felt cold. At long last, sunset, and our preparations were as finished as we could make them. Dressed in a soldier's uniform, my hair cut short under my cap, my chest wrapped tight to make me look more like a man, I stood inspection in front of Carlos, trying to still my feverish shivering.

Looking very handsome and official in his officer's uniform, he nodded his approval and said, "Remember, we are from Suales. It's far enough from here I don't think anyone will ask any questions, but don't say a word. You are my aide, nobody of importance. I will do all the talking."

I nodded. Carlos handed me some coca leaves. This

time I took them without objection, praying they'd keep me going. *Just let me get Trevor free. Then I can collapse.* Ignoring the fever-ache in my bones, I marched — tottered — behind Carlos toward the fortress.

At the gate, Carlos pounded and shouted, but no one came. Glancing both ways to be sure we were unobserved, he produced a key and, after a few nerve-wracking failures, got the gate open. Closing it carefully behind us, but leaving it unlocked, Carlos gestured to me to follow him as he marched purposefully through the front doors and paused in the hallway. It was a scene from the last act of *Macbeth*. Bodies lay everywhere; a few of them, semi-conscious, groaned, but nobody was alert enough to ask us who we were. A few were covered with vomit; the stench was appalling. With a cautious glance around the hall, Carlos headed for the stairway with me trailing behind him, fighting a lethargy that made me want to lie down and sleep. But the coca leaves gave me a little strength.

On the second floor, there was no one in sight at all. On the third floor, a young soldier raised his head and tried to shout a challenge, but Carlos clubbed him with a pistol before he could make a sound. Exhausted, I stumbled up the last flight of stairs behind my "superior officer". He put his mouth next to my ear and whispered. "The keys are probably on somebody's belt. Find them. Hurry!"

The cell doors were heavy wood with a small barred window in each, and he moved off, running lightly, glancing into each cell. I hurried across the hall, glancing at belts, wondering if the keys would be in someone's pocket, not looking forward to having to search each body individually. I realized I hadn't asked Carlos if the drugged soldiers would recover or die — but I didn't care. All I wanted to do was find Trevor and get out of this place.

I found a large ring of keys hanging on a hook above

a table at the far end of the hall near another staircase. Cautiously I approached the soldier slumped across the table, who groaned and opened his eyes. "Who th' fug'r you?"

"Orders from Ortiz," I murmured, trying to make my voice as deep as possible. "Moving the *gringo*."

I reached for the keys, but he grabbed my arm and dragged me back. His breath smelled of vomit and liquor. "Ain't never seen you before. Whose orders?"

I forced myself to smile. "Heh, *amigo*, you don't look so good." I touched his face, moving my hand up to grab his hair. "You okay?"

The soldier opened his mouth to answer, but by that time my knife blade was deep in his larynx. His eyes bulging, he grabbed his throat and tried to shout, but his blood gushed down the front of his uniform and spilled warm over my hand as I snatched the keys and tried to retrieve my knife. It was lodged in his throat, stuck between his twitching fingers. Panicking, I jerked it free, dragging the soldier's body off the chair onto the floor. I turned to find Carlos waving to me. "I found him," he whispered. "Come quickly."

Fever and exhaustion forgotten, I sped back across the hall. Trevor was peering out the cell window, his hair dirty and matted, calling softly, "Here! Hurry!"

It felt like forever before Carlos found the right key, while Trevor and I stared hungrily at each other through the bars. "Daphne? Is that really you?" Then I was in his arms, both of us crying and laughing.

"Enough!" Carlos hissed. "We must move!"

Nodding to Carlos, Trevor stooped to snatch a gun from one of the unconscious soldiers and I was relieved to see he appeared to be okay physically, although his face was haggard and he had lost a lot of weight. I pulled my own gun, hoping I would be able to use it — it felt as if it weighed at least three tons — and Trevor grabbed my other hand. I breathed a sigh of relief as we raced down the last flight of stairs — only to be confronted by three soldiers who had apparently just arrived. Their guns came up, but Carlos was faster, spraying them with his automatic rifle. They fell back against the door, but suddenly bullets were coming from behind us. Trevor turned and shot the attacker, but the man got off one more round before he fell and I felt something hit me in the right shoulder as I raced after Carlos and Trevor. With their longer legs, they were at the gate long before I stumbled up to it.

The shooting must have awakened some of the soldiers, because a few staggered out the fortress door just as we slammed the gate. Trevor motioned for Carlos and me to go on, then took careful aim between the bars of the gate. I heard several shots and suddenly Trevor was thundering just behind me. We raced for the woods where Carlos and I had hidden our shoulder packs.

My eyes not yet used to the darkness, I stumbled and yelped when Trevor grabbed my arm. "What's wrong?" he asked.

"I think I've been hit," I replied. My shoulder was numb and my head swam. In the dim light between trees, Carlos examined my shoulder quickly.

"Only a flesh wound," he whispered, still speaking Queterá "We must get far from here as fast as possible."

I translated for Trevor and we set off at a trot. So far there had been no sound of pursuit, but that wouldn't last. Blessedly, it started to rain, and Carlos, a dark shadow among shadows ahead of us, slipped ghostlike through the trees. Trevor and I hurried to catch up.

I stuffed coca leaves into my mouth and handed some to Trevor. "Like it or not, they've kept me going," I told him. "You'd better do the same."

Without a word he put the leaves in his mouth and bit off the stems.

Vehicles roared to life on the road behind us. "They won't be able to drive in the thickest parts of the forest,"

Carlos told us. "But they'll spread out on foot. Hurry!"

Again I translated for Trevor, who wisely asked no questions, and we increased our pace. The rain came down harder, and all of us slipped and fell several times. My shoulder felt numb until I landed on it, and then I had all I could do to keep from screaming aloud. Trevor grabbed my other arm and we hurried on, dodging branches, slipping, sliding, swearing, always aware of the shouts of the soldiers behind us. A thornbush caught at my sleeve, clawing long gashes in my arm. And I was tired — so tired. My boots seemed to be made of concrete; my side ached and my shoulder pack felt as if it were full of lead. Trevor finally took it from me and slipped his arm around my waist. "C'mon, my love. We have a wedding to go to, and we're not gonna be late."

I have no idea how we got to the river so fast, although I was vaguely aware we'd taken a much more direct route than the one Carlos and I had taken coming in. Suddenly a rope bridge was in front of us, stretched across the narrows, the river swollen and thundering beneath it, the planks wet and slippery. Whitewater gleamed in the faint light, sloshing across the bridge. Carlos glanced at us, then started carefully across. Trevor pushed me ahead. "Go on. I'll be right behind you." I inched across, nursing my wounded arm, trying not to look at the river pounding on the rocks below me. *Juanito, you made it. Help me now!* Suddenly there was a shout from the bank, just as my foot slipped and pitched me into the water. Trevor grabbed my collar, but the current was too strong and I felt my shirt rip as I was dragged deeper into the turbulence. The icy water made my whole body ache. I surfaced once and heard a distant shout, but as I was pulled under again, my lungs bursting, I knew that the Woman of Ice and Snow had accomplished her task in this lifetime.

It was so easy then to let go and let the blackness take me.

Suddenly I was floating above the trees on the other side of the river. Below me Trevor and Carlos were in heated argument, Trevor obviously wanting to go back to rescue me, Carlos insisting they must go on.

Trevor pulled out of Carlos' grasp and ran back toward the river, his eyes searching hungrily. But Carlos dragged Trevor away, snarling something in Spanish. Soldiers on the opposite bank opened fire and a few of them started across the rope bridge just as it was ripped from its moorings by the torrent.

Trevor raised his head and stared straight at me, his eyes full of anguish and longing. "Daphne!" he shouted.

I waved him on and blew a final kiss as Carlos dragged him into the woods. *Blue skies, my love, fair winds. We almost made it. I'll see you next time around!* Near the river, the soldiers stopped, staring uncertainly at the raging river, and the only sound was the rain and the thundering whitewater.

21

Trevor's Story

I'd never known such agony, grabbing for Daphne, feeling her slip out of my grasp. She surfaced once, and then was gone. Already across the river, her friend called urgently, *"¡Prisa, señor!"*

I moved as quickly as I could across the rapidly weakening bridge, my eyes straining for some sign of Daphne. Ahead of me, my guide was racing away from the river.

"Wait!" I shouted. "We have to find her!"

"Señor, you will not find her alive. She would want you to go on without her."

"No! I have to go back!"

He grabbed my arm. "The soldiers are behind us! We cannot wait any longer!"

I jerked free. "We can't leave her! Maybe she surfaced downstream." I ran back toward the river, but he grabbed my arm and pulled me away, shouting that soldiers were aiming at us from the opposite bank. I realized some of the "rain" I was hearing were bullets. He was much stronger than I was, and shoved me roughly toward the trees.

Suddenly I heard Daphne's voice, seeming to come from above my head. I couldn't make out the words, but I saw her for a moment, floating above the treetops, almost transparent, motioning for me to go on. "Daphne!" I cried. But she waved and blew me a kiss as my guide grabbed my arm again and dragged me into the woods.

Unable to speak, I lurched after my strange companion as he marched ahead, apparently understanding I needed time. The rain slacked off, finally stopping about midnight. As the moon slid from behind a cloud, we paused under a tree to rest and he turned dark sad eyes on me.

"My name is Carlos Sánchez," he said softly. "My father makes furniture which your lady sold for him in the U.S."

"I guess I should thank you for rescuing me, but we should have tried harder to rescue *her. . .*"

"*Señor,* I understand. But I must tell you that she knew she would not live through this."

"She told you that?"

"She did not actually say it, but she knew. My father also knew, and tried to tell her. She told me it did not matter — all that mattered was getting you out."

I stared out at the night, rain sparkling on leaves in the moonlight. Daphne would have loved it. The tears came then, and I made no attempt to hide them.

Carlos waited patiently. "She was a very special lady, *señor*. I did not realize how special until now. She did some very foolish things, but I see now how much she loved you. She told me you write and take pictures. You must write of this, my friend. You must tell what you have seen and heard."

"There's so much I don't know. How did you find me? Why did she come down here? The damned, wonderful fool. . ."

"I will tell you, my friend, and you will write it."

And so we walked through the night, as Carlos told me about the last days of my beloved.

Epilogue

ASSOCIATED PRESS, NEW YORK — Friends gathered at the Four Seasons restaurant today to celebrate photojournalist Trevor West Elliot's receipt of the Pulitzer Prize for Non-fiction for his book, Nueva Sangria: The Land Nobody Wanted, *an exposé of the turbulent politics in that South American country. The book chronicles Elliot's investigation into the political corruption and bloody war for land rights between coca growers and oil barons, exacerbated by the USDEA's push to eradicate coca plantations altogether.*

"I couldn't have written it without the help of my dear friend Carlos Sánchez and the lady whose love will live in my memory forever: Daphne Morris." Elliot frequently fought tears during his acceptance speech.

While researching his book, Elliot was kidnapped by the Nueva Sangrian regime and held for ransom. Morris, aided by Sánchez, succeeded in a heroic rescue of Elliot but drowned during their escape. She and Elliot had planned to marry upon his return from Nueva Sangria. Elliot dedicated his prize-winning book to her memory.

Did you enjoy this book?
Spread the news!
Log in to Amazon.com and
write a review!

About the Author

Jonni Anderson has been writing since she knew what a pencil was for, even before she knew what those squiggles meant. "I never had any desire to be anything but a writer," she says. Anderson has written plays, short stories, poetry, and newspaper articles, as well as several novels.

She has worked in the administration end of the construction industry, traveled internationally for a government contractor, and now lives in Florida where she is an editor and POD book designer.

Two of her novels, *Cranwold* and *The Other Side of Time,* are currently available from Amazon.com, Kobo.com, Barnes & Noble and other retailers. Many of her short stories are also available for Kindle at Amazon.com.

She welcomes comments from her readers and can be reached through her website, jonnianderson.com. Her book layout and design business is at starwatchcreations.com.